Pulse

WEST
DUNBARTONSHIRE
LIBRARIES

PRICE	SUPPLIER
£2.81	AM
LOCATION	CLASS
DP	JF
INVOICE DATE	
27.4.11	
ACCESSION NUMBER	
C020345635	

Annabelle Starr

EGMONT

Special thanks to:

Kirsty Neale, St John's Walworth Church of England School
and Belmont Primary School

EGMONT
We bring stories to life

Pulse first published in Great Britain 2008
by Egmont UK Limited
239 Kensington High Street, London W8 6SA

Text & illustration © 2008 Egmont UK Ltd
Text by Kirsty Neale
Illustrations by Helen Turner

ISBN 978 1 4052 3931 8

1 3 5 7 9 10 8 6 4 2

A CIP catalogue record for this title is available
from the British Library

Typeset by Avon DataSet Ltd, Bidford on Avon, Warwickshire
Printed and bound in Great Britain by the CPI Group

All rights reserved. No part of this publication may be reproduced,
stored in a retrieval system, or transmitted, in any form or by
any means, electronic, mechanical, photocopying, recording
or otherwise, without the prior permission of the publisher.

'The books were great – I want to read the next ones!'
Abbie, age 8

'I read them really quickly because I wanted
to know what happened next'
Robin, age 9

'I didn't want to put the books down – I just wanted
to carry on reading!'
Harriet, age 9

'I liked the fact file and quizzes at the back and the
phrasebook at the beginning'
Lucy, age 11

'*Megastar Mysteries* is really cool. I can't wait to read more!'
Ciara, age 10

'I liked that I knew something was happening
but I didn't know what until the end'
Lydia, age 10

We want to know what *you* think about
Megastar Mysteries! Visit:

www.mega-star.co.uk

for loads of coolissimo megastar
stuff to do!

Meet the
Megastar Mysteries Team!

Hi, I'm **Rosie Parker** (the one with the mystery radar extraordinaire), and these are my fab friends . . .

. . . **Soph** (Sophie) **McCoy**, schoolgirl by day, budding fashion designer by night (and at weekends) . . .

. . . and **Abs** (Abigail) **Flynn** – in brief, she's brainissimo!

This is my mum, **Liz Parker**, owner of the dodgiest outfits ever known to womankind, and creator of the even dodgier Bananarama tribute band, the Banana Splits . . .

. . . and this is my nan, **Pam Parker**, biscuit fiend and murder-mystery show fanatic. She's always full of ideas, and some of them are actually good.

Consider yourself introduced!

ROSIE'S MINI MEGASTAR PHRASEBOOK

Want to speak our lingo, but don't know your soeurs from your signorinas? No problemo! Just use my comprehensive guide . . .

-a-rama	add this ending to a word to indicate a large quantity: e.g. 'The after-show party was celeb-a-rama'
amigo	Spanish for 'friend'
au contraire, mon frère	French for 'on the contrary, my brother'
au revoir	French for 'goodbye'
barf/barfy/barfissimo	sick/sick-making/very sick-making indeed
bien sûr, ma soeur	French for 'of course, my sister'
bon	French for 'good'
bonjour	French for 'hello'
celeb	short for 'celebrity'
convo	short for 'conversation'
cringe-fest	a highly embarrassing situation
Cringeville	a place we all visit from time to time when something truly embarrassing happens to us
cringeworthy	an embarrassing person, place or thing might be described as this
daggy	Australian for 'unfashionable' or 'unstylish'
doco	short for 'documentary'
exactamundo	not a real foreign word, but a great way to express your agreement with someone
exactement	French for 'exactly'

excusez moi	French for 'excuse me'
fashionista	'a keen follower of fashion' – can be teamed with 'sista' for added rhyming fun
glam	short for 'glamorous'
gorge/gorgey	short for 'gorgeous': e.g. 'the lead singer of that band is gorge/gorgey'
hilarioso	not a foreign word at all, just a great way to liven up 'hilarious'
hola, señora	Spanish for 'hello, missus'
hottie	no, this is *not* short for hot water bottle – it's how you might describe an attractive-looking boy to your friends
-issimo	try adding this ending to English adjectives for extra emphasis: e.g. coolissimo, crazissimo – très funissimo, non?
je ne sais pas	French for 'I don't know'
je voudrais un beau garçon, s'il vous plaît	French for 'I would like an attractive boy, please'
journos	short for 'journalists'
les Français	French for, erm, 'the French'
Loserville	this is where losers live, particularly evil school bully Amanda Hawkins
mais	French for 'but'
marvelloso	not technically a foreign word, just a more exotic version of 'marvellous'
massivo	Italian for 'massive'
mon amie/mes amis	French for 'my friend'/'my friends'
muchos	Spanish for 'many'

non	French for 'no'
nous avons deux garçons ici	French for 'we have two boys here'
no way, José!	'that's never going to happen!'
oui	French for 'yes'
quelle horreur!	French for 'what horror!'
quelle surprise!	French for 'what a surprise!'
sacrebleu	French for 'gosh' or even 'blimey'
stupido	this is the Italian for 'stupid' – stupid!
-tastic	add this ending to any word to indicate a lot of something: e.g. 'Abs is braintastic'
très	French for 'very'
swoonsome	decidedly attractive
si, si, signor/signorina	Italian for 'yes, yes, mister/miss'
terriblement	French for 'terribly'
une grande	French for 'a big' – add the word 'genius' and you have the perfect description of Abs
Vogue	it's only the world's most influential fashion magazine, darling!
voilà	French for 'there it is'
what's the story, Rory?	'what's going on?'
what's the plan, Stan?	'which course of action do you think we should take?'
what the crusty old grandads?	'what on earth?'
zut alors!	French for 'darn it!'

Hi Megastar reader!

My name's Annabelle Starr*. I'm a fashion stylist – just like Soph's Aunt Penny – which means it's my job to help celebrities look their best at all times.

Over the years, I've worked with all sorts of big names, some of whom also have seriously big egos! Take the time I flew all theway to Japan to style a shoot for a girl band. One of the members refused to wear the designer number I'd picked out for her and insisted on sporting a dress her mum had run up from some revolting old curtains instead. The only way I could get her to take it off was to persuade her it didn't match her pet Pekingese's outfit!

Anyway, when I first started out, I never dreamt I'd write a series of books based around my crazy celebrity experiences, but that's just what I've done with Megastar Mysteries. Rosie, Soph and Abs have just the sort of adventures I wish my friends and I could have got up to when we were teenagers!

I really hope you enjoy reading the books as much as I enjoyed writing them!

Love *Annabelle*

* I'll let you in to a little secret: this isn't my real name, but in this business you can never be too careful!

Chapter One

If there's one good thing about the drama lessons at our dull school, it's that they're not the science lessons at our dull school. Really – that's as good as it gets. This is partly down to the teachers. Mr Lord – Time Lord, as we call him – is our so-called drama teacher, although he mostly just goes on about how he once played a Cyberman in *Doctor Who*. Our science teacher, Mr Footer, is in training for the title of World's Most Boring Man, and he's doing very well. He also has a moustache that looks like a slug. It's the slug that clinches things in the rubbish-teacher stakes, but it's a close-run thing.

So when Time Lord stood smugly in front of our drama class one Monday morning and said he'd got an important announcement to make, nobody exactly sat up and looked interested. Not that a bunch of bored faces ever stopped Time Lord from droning on before.

'As most of you will remember, I trained at an excellent drama school before joining the cast of *Doctor Who*, followed by a number of other challenging stage and television roles,' he began.

'That'll be "excellent", meaning the only place that'd take him,' whispered my best mate, Abs, who was sitting next to me and my other best friend, Soph, near the back of the drama studio.

'And "a number of" meaning two,' I added.

We sniggered as Time Lord carried on.

'One of my fellow graduates, Jim Falconer, is a filmmaker, and he's been looking for a location for his latest project, *Pulse*. Naturally, I was one of the first people he called for advice and, thanks to my

years of experience in the world of film and television, I was able to help him out. The film is a musical, written by Jim himself,' he added, going into what Abs calls his 'actor-mode'. He basically gets all over-dramatic with this wild, looking-into-the-distance expression and lots of long pauses. It's mucho hilarioso. 'It's a classic story of misguided youths, a passionate, brilliant teacher and how even the greatest of problems can be solved through music and dance.'

Good grief.

'A group of unruly pupils,' said Time Lord, seeming to squint in my direction, 'are thrown together by their headmistress to organise a school dance, in a last-ditch attempt to stop their bad behaviour. Rivalry, love interest,' he went on, 'it's all there.'

He looked around the room, obviously expecting us to be enthralled or impressed or something. No one was. He carried on, a bit less actor-ish now, but still with this mega-smug expression on his face.

'Anyway, once Jim had filled me in on the details, I had a brainwave. As it was set in a school, Whitney High would be the perfect location! I could be his inside man, and even take on one of the film's smaller – but most vital – roles. Strictly as a favour to an old friend,' he added, hastily.

'How much d'you reckon he begged?' Soph said under her breath.

'Bribed, more like,' I grinned.

'Jim jumped at the chance to offer me a part in his film, as well as using Whitney High as the location,' Time Lord finished.

This was starting to sound way cooler than the stuff he normally comes up with. Exactly fourteen people saw our last play (it was about a misunderstood mushroom farmer), and I'm pretty sure Time Lord paid most of them to turn up. Even Mum and Nan – who'll usually sit through any old rubbish – made excuses not to come.

'They're going to make a film in our school?' said Abs, doubtfully. It did seem too good to be true.

'Not just a film, Miss Flynn – a musical,' said Time Lord, dreamily. 'I've always been a big fan, myself. *West Side Story*, *Guys and Dolls*, *My Fair Lady* – all the greats. I was once likened to a young Gene Kelly by a reviewer in the *Biddlesbury Reporter*, you know.'

'Where's Biddlesbury?' asked Abs.

'And who's Gene Kelly?' said Soph.

Time Lord looked totally shocked.

'Who's Gene Kelly?' he echoed. 'Surely you've seen *Singin' in the Rain*?'

He stared around the group and we all shook our heads blankly.

Five things that happened in the next twenty minutes:

1. Time Lord gave us a lecture on this actor, Gene Kelly, and a bunch of other film stars who are now either very old or very dead.

2. Time Lord filled us in on the entire plot of *Singin' in the Rain* (so there's no point in

actually watching it now, cos we know exactly what happens).

3. Time Lord borrowed Frankie Gabriel's umbrella.

4. Time Lord and Frankie Gabriel's umbrella demonstrated the famous scene where Gene Kelly sings and dances in the rain.

5. Time Lord leaned on Frankie Gabriel's umbrella to kick his tap-dancing feet up in the air. Frankie Gabriel's umbrella broke. Possibly one of Time Lord's toes did, too.

'As I was saying,' puffed Time Lord, hobbling back to his desk, 'I was one of the few pupils at the Elizabeth Meakins School of Dance and Drama who could sing, dance and act, all at the same time. It's a skill very few performers ever perfect, but those of us who have it feel obliged to share it every once in a while.'

Seriously, it can't be good to hold in a laugh as big as the one I was stifling. I made the massivo mistake of looking at Abs and nearly exploded.

I turned my spluttering into a coughing fit and Soph thumped me on the back.

'Is there a problem, Rosie?' said Time Lord.

'We were just wondering, sir,' Abs managed to squeak, 'if you know who'll be appearing in *Pulse*?'

'Well, Jim's keeping most of the stars' identities a secret until we start filming,' he said, clearly enjoying the fact we actually seemed interested in what he was saying for once. 'But I've already let slip that yours truly will be amongst the big names on set, and a little show-business bird told me Estelle Mayor will be joining us, too.'

'Estelle!' said Soph.

'You might remember her from the television talent show, *Stage-Struck*,' said Time Lord.

Well, duh! We might also remember her from the time me, Abs and Soph reunited her with her mum's famous long-lost brother on live TV in yet another triumph of mystery-solving genius.

'There's also the chance for a few of Whitney High's most talented drama students to join the cast as extras,' Time Lord continued. 'And as this is a low-budget movie, Jim might need the extras to help with the props as well.'

There was a definite hum of excitement in the air now. I grinned at Abs and Soph. We sooo had to do it!

Time Lord raised his voice. 'For those of you who are interested, I'll be holding auditions next week, although,' he added, looking at Amanda Hawkins with a barf-making smile, 'these will merely be a formality for some people.'

Amanda is totally Time Lord's pet pupil, as well as being my sworn enemy and the class witch. She gets the lead in every play we do, even though she's useless and can't act her way out of a carrier bag. But no way was I going to let Amanda Hawkins ruin news like this.

'This is the single most exciting thing ever to happen at Whitney High,' I said to Soph and Abs the minute our lesson ended.

'This is the ONLY exciting thing ever to happen here,' Abs corrected me. 'We *are* going to audition, right?'

'Do the French eat frogs' legs?' I said. 'After all, we've been extras before. We've got *experience*.' Me, Abs and Soph had worked on a film set once, and ended up making a blink-and-you'll-miss-it appearance in the background of one of the scenes.

'That was just standing around though, not singing and dancing. We'll have to pick something to sing for the audition,' said Abs.

'And a dance routine,' I agreed.

'Clothes!' said Soph.

'Yeah, I was thinking I'd wear some,' I said.

'You can't just *wear* them,' she said, sounding horrified. 'There's all the thinking about them, and making new stuff. And we've only got a week!'

Soph, in case it's not stunningly obvious, is obsessed with fashion.

* * *

By the end of the week, the entire school was buzzing with news, gossip and wild rumours about the filming. A girl from year eleven swore she'd overheard Time Lord telling Madame Bertillon, our French teacher, that Orlando Bloom was actually a brilliant singer and dancer and was starring in *Pulse* so he could finally reveal this to the world. Becky Blakeney, who's in the same form as me and Soph, told us she'd heard one of the stars had left to join a death-metal band and they were planning to pick a replacement from the people who went to Time Lord's auditions. Just when you thought it couldn't get any weirder, Luke Bailey from year ten started saying Jim Falconer didn't exist and it was actually Time Lord (in disguise) who was going to be making the film.

'Yeah, right,' scoffed Abs, 'as if Time Lord's a good enough actor to pull *that* off.'

'You know what *is* true, though?' said Soph. The three of us had just plonked ourselves down in our usual seats in the canteen, and Soph was as desperate as I was to tell Abs the juicy bit of gossip we'd overheard at morning break. 'Amanda

Hawkins is having extra coaching sessions every lunchtime.'

'Drama coaching,' I added, just to make sure Abs understood the enormousness of the news. 'With Time Lord.'

'No *way*!' Abs's jaw practically hit her plate.

I nodded, quite smugly. Gossip rocks.

'How is that fair?' said Abs. 'Why should Amanda Hawkins get more of a chance than the rest of us?'

'That's what we thought at first,' said Soph, 'but then Rosie pointed out –'

'– Time Lord's not exactly wowing big movie producers at auditions every day of the week,' I finished.

'He might wreck Amanda's chances instead of improving them,' said Soph.

A surprisingly evil grin spread over Abs's face. 'Oui, oui, mes amis. You might just be right.'

'Hey, who's that with Meanie Greenie?' I said, as our headmistress came into the canteen with a tall, scruffy-looking man.

'Ladies and gentlemen,' shouted Mrs Green, before Abs or Soph had chance to answer. She clapped her hands and the canteen fell silent. 'As I'm sure you're aware, Whitney High is to be used as the setting for a film during our summer break this year. Earlier today, I had the pleasure of meeting Mr Falconer, the film's director,' – she gestured at the scruffy man – 'who's here to look around. In order to clear up some of the silly stories and rumours we seem to have fallen prey to over the last few days,' she continued, raising her eyebrows in a way you could totally tell meant 'bonkeroonie lies', 'Mr Falconer has kindly agreed to stay on and answer students' questions in the main hall after lunch. I suggest you think about what you'd like to ask him.'

She swept out of the room with Jim Falconer (who clearly wasn't Time Lord in disguise) hot on her clacking heels.

'Blimey,' said Abs.

'You know what this means?' I said.

'Yep. First period maths is cancelled,' Soph nodded.

I leant back in my chair, grinning. This film thing was just getting better and better!

'Of course, some of us have already met him,' I heard a voice saying behind me.

'Was that in your private coaching lesson?' said another voice.

I kept completely still in my leaning-back position. It was seriously uncomfortable, but I'm always prepared to suffer for nosiness.

'Yep. Time Lord introduced me as his star pupil,' said the first voice. Amanda Hawkins. What joy. 'He had to cut our session short for today because he had important stuff to discuss with Jim.'

'Like what?' said someone else. Considering Amanda wasn't calling them names, insulting their parents or trying to nick their lunch money, I guessed the other two voices belonged to her vile-issimo cronies, Lara Neils and Keira Roberts.

'Well,' said Amanda, 'I couldn't hang around for long, but I did hear them talking about who's going to be in the film. As well as Estelle Mayor, there's going to be another girl and two boys.'

Four film stars actually here in our school for, like, the entire summer! I sooo had to ace the audition and become an extra!

'Did he say who they were?' asked Lara. Or maybe Keira.

'Oh, yeah,' said Amanda, and I heard a chair scraping. 'Come on, I feel like a bit of fresh air. I'll tell you outside.'

I leant back as far as I could, straining to hear if Amanda said anything else as they walked out. A second later, I was flat on my back with my legs in the air, showing my knickers to half the canteen.

'Did you see that?' I said, as Abs and Soph helped me out of my tipped-over chair.

'Yeah,' said Soph. 'Your knickers sooo don't match your uniform.'

'Not that,' I said, a bit red in the face. 'Amanda. D'you think they saw me ear-wigging?'

'Totally,' said Abs.

But I never say never when it comes to fishing for celeb gossip. There was something juicy to be uncovered, and I just had to find out what.

Chapter Two

'Come on,' I said to Abs and Soph, pushing my lunch tray away.

'Where?' said Soph.

'Don't do it,' Abs warned.

'Do what?'

'Follow Amanda.'

I raised one eyebrow. It's a très amusing skill I've been practising in front of the mirror for nearly a month now. I have to kind of twitch my nose to make it work, but it annoys people (Mum, Time Lord, Abs) so much, it's totally worth it.

'Who says I'm going to follow Amanda?' I said indignantly.

'Aren't you?' said Abs.

'I'm not, actually,' I said in my best snooty voice. 'I've got some homework I want to make a start on.'

'Really?' said Soph.

I swung my bag over my shoulder. 'Nope. I'm going after Amanda. Come on.'

By the time we found Amanda and her cronies sitting outside the science block, Abs had more or less stopped muttering about how my nosiness was practically a disease, and I'd come up with a plan.

'Be nice,' I hissed to the others as we walked towards Amanda.

OK, so it wasn't the *best* plan. None of us can stand Amanda, but I didn't get to be Second Mushroom in our last school play without knowing how to act.

'Hey,' I said, sitting on the wall a little way away from her.

'Are you talking to me?' sneered Amanda.

'Chewing gum?' I offered her the packet I'd just pulled out of my bag.

'This is a trick, right?' said Amanda. 'It's bogey-flavoured or something.'

I shook my head. 'I'm just trying to be friendly.'

She looked a bit suspicious, then took three pieces of gum and handed one each to Lara and Keira.

'So, how come you were late for lunch?' I said as casually as I could.

'Drama coaching,' said Amanda.

'Cool,' I said, nudging Abs and Soph, who made agreeing noises. 'For the auditions?'

Amanda nodded.

'I still can't believe we get to perform in front of a *real* film director,' I said.

'It's no big deal,' said Amanda. 'People get so hung up about celebrities and stuff.'

'I know,' I said. 'It's like Estelle – she was completely normal and cool when we met her on *Stage-Struck*.'

'Yeah?'

'Totally. Hey, we'll introduce you, if you like.'

'Wow,' said Amanda. 'Really?'

'Course,' I grinned.

Am I a genius or what? Amanda was totally softening up. I took a deep breath and went for the killer question.

'I don't s'pose you've heard who else is in the film? Apart from you and Estelle, I mean.'

Amanda bit her lip and leaned forward in a gossip-ahoy kind of way.

'I probably shouldn't tell you this,' she said, 'but when I was in the drama studio before, Jim Falconer was there. You know, the director.'

'Go on,' I breathed.

'He was talking to Time Lord about who's in the film. I definitely overheard Estelle's name and then –'

She looked around to check the coast was clear before going on.

'– he said no way was he going to let nosy parkers, fashion freaks or speccy swots ruin his film.'

Amanda and her cronies collapsed laughing.

'You should see your face,' she said, pointing at me between laughs. 'Did you really think I'd fall for that pathetic "being friendly" act? Talk about desperate.'

'Let's go,' said Abs, standing up.

'I bet you were hoping for some kind of celebrity scoop for that stupid magazine you're always sucking up to. Lame or what?' She turned to Lara and Keira.

'Lamer than a lame person being, like, totally lame,' said Lara, who is mind-bogglingly thick.

'Er, hello?' I said. '*Star Secrets* is not a stupid magazine, and I don't suck up to them, I –'

But Abs grabbed my arm and pulled me away.

'Not worth it,' she said, quietly. 'They won't listen anyway.'

'Swot-girl's right,' said Amanda. 'Haven't you lot got a rock somewhere you can go and crawl back under?'

'You'd know all about rocks,' I shouted over my shoulder – Abs and Soph were practically dragging me away now. 'Your head's full of them.'

I was sooo going to get her back for this.

✳ ✳ ✳

Thanks to my brain, which is almost as brilliant as Abs's when it comes to stuff like revenge and celeb gossip – although, sadly not lessons – it only took me until the next morning to come up with a totally excellent idea.

'Genius plan alert,' I announced to Abs and Soph at the beginning of lunch.

They looked at me suspiciously.

'Does it involve me getting called "Swot-girl" again?' said Abs.

'Or me having to look at Keira Roberts's socks, which, like, totally clash with her uniform?' said Soph.

'Au contraire, mes sensitive frères. We,' I announced, 'are getting extra drama coaching from Time Lord.'

Abs's eyes went all squinty and narrow. 'What?'

'Drama coaching. I asked him this morning. He said to come along at lunchtime.'

'You are joking,' said Soph.

'Think about it,' I said. 'The drama studio is *the* best place for overhearing gossip about the film.'

'I do like gossip,' said Soph.

'If we found out something Amanda didn't know, we could so get back at her,' I said.

Abs looked a bit doubtful, but then seemed to give in. 'It had better be seriously good gossip to make it worth putting up with Time Lord,' she said.

'Film stars in our school,' I said. 'How can that not be good gossip?'

✳ ✳ ✳

Five minutes later we were in the drama studio, listening to one of Time Lord's famous lectures.

'I'm thrilled you're taking this so seriously,' he said. 'Of course, with my more talented students, extra coaching is the icing on the cake, to make sure they shine at the auditions. You three, on the other hand . . . well, let's just say there's plenty of progress to be made. Being an extra isn't as easy as some people might think.'

Abs shot me a seriously evil look as he started wittering on about his favourite subject – *Doctor Who*. I wondered how we could get him to start spilling what he knew about the film.

'Sir,' I said when he paused for breath. 'Is there anything else you can tell us about the film? I mean, who the main characters are, the actors . . . You know, background information, so we can get into the right mood when we're auditioning.'

Convincing or what? Honestly, I don't think there's much Time Lord can teach me.

'Excellent question,' he beamed. 'I was talking to Jim about this the other day. At drama school, he often turned to me for advice before auditions, and now I'm passing that same invaluable information on to students who audition for him. Funny, eh? Back then, I was like a mentor to him. If it wasn't for my encouragement, he might still be a mere extra himself.'

And on and on he went for the *entire* hour. Cybermen, drama school and blowing his own trumpet. So much for coaching and, more to the point, finding out anything about the film.

* * *

'I wonder if Time Lord spends all of Amanda's coaching sessions talking about himself,' I said, as the three of us sat reading the latest issue of *Star Secrets* a few days later.

It was Saturday afternoon, and we were hanging out at my house. Nan was at Trotters, the café on the high street, with one of her friends, so for once we had the lounge to ourselves.

'You do realise,' said Abs, 'we've spent three très yawnsome lunchtimes in drama coaching this week, and we still don't know what we're singing at the auditions.'

'It's a nightmare,' Soph agreed. 'I can't design our outfits until I know.'

'Ooh, outfits for what?' said a voice, and I nearly fell off the sofa in shock. Mum was meant to be upstairs using my computer to update the website for her tragic eighties tribute band, the Banana Splits, not downstairs listening in on convos that were definitely not for her ears.

'Nothing,' I said.

'Film auditions,' said Soph at the same time.

Bum and pants and zut alors.

'Auditions?' said Mum. 'What film?'

'*Pulse*,' said Soph before I could shove a cushion in her mouth. 'You know, the musical they're filming at school over the summer.'

'They're making a film at Whitney High? A musical?' said Mum.

'Yeah,' said Soph, giving me a funny look. I desperately tried to signal 'shut up, you loon' with my eyes, but it didn't work. 'I thought Rosie would've mentioned it. We're auditioning to be extras.'

Mum looked like her head was about to explode with excitement, which was precisely why

I hadn't told her about it.

'When?' she asked.

'The week after next. Time Lord's giving us extra coaching,' I added, pretty sure I knew what was coming next.

'But it's a musical,' she said. 'I'm sure Mr Lord knows all about acting, but what about singing and dancing?'

I opened my mouth to explain about the Elizabeth Meakins School of Dance and Drama, then thought better of it.

'What you need is someone who can sing and dance, someone who really knows how to *perform* on stage,' said Mum.

'If only we knew someone like that,' I muttered. Abs giggled.

'Soph, help me move this table out of the way,' Mum commanded. 'Rosie, you and Abs push the sofa right back against the wall.'

'Mum,' I protested.

'No need to thank me,' she said. 'What sort of mother would I be if I didn't help my only child?

Now, if you're going to be ready for this audition,' she continued, still heaving furniture about, 'we need to be organised. A true professional works night and day to perfect their act. If you want to be the best, you've got to walk the walk and talk the talk.'

She stood back to admire the space she'd cleared.

'Well, it's not a dance studio, but it'll do. Shoes off, girls – get ready to warm up.'

'Mum,' I said, gritting my teeth, 'who said we need help with the audition?'

'Well, Abs said you didn't know what you were doing and Soph said that was why she couldn't start on the outfits yet.'

I glared at Abs, who suddenly seemed very interested in untying the laces on her trainers.

'We'll work something out,' I said, but Mum ignored me and started rifling through her enormous collection of eighties CDs.

'Talking of outfits, I'm seeing fuschia-coloured unitards,' she said. 'You know, those all-in-one leotard-and-tights things? And then little grey jersey skirts over the top, with legwarmers and headbands in neon pink.'

Soph gave me an alarmed look.

'A-ha!' Mum cried, finding the CD she was looking for. A second later, 'Jump' was blaring out of the lounge speakers. Only it wasn't the quite-good-actually Girls Aloud version.

'No way,' I shouted over the noise.

'What?' said Mum, who was doing some seriously terrible moves, working out the start of a dance routine.

'No way are we auditioning to this song,' I said.

'You like it. I've heard you playing it upstairs,' shouted Mum.

'That's the Girls Aloud version,' I yelled back.

'The original's much better,' she said, clicking her fingers and doing a twiddly dance step to the left. 'They don't make them like this any more.'

'There's a reason for that,' I said darkly.

'Fine,' she said. 'We'll use the Girls Aloud version. You go and get it, and we'll start our warm-up down here. First step on the path to showbiz success,' she added, winking at Soph and Abs.

I gave in. She's like an all-singing, all-dancing, legwarmer-obsessed bulldozer. And even though it was très annoying, I had to admit she was right on the needing-a-song front. Time Lord had been no help at all. At least now we might stand a chance of getting through the auditions. As I headed upstairs to get my Girls Aloud CD, I heard her shout, 'That's it, Soph – shimmy, shimmy! Let me see those jazz-hands, Abs.'

I may have to emigrate when all this is over.

Pulse Auditions – rehearse schedule
(as drawn up by Liz Parker)
Auditionees: Rosie, Soph, Abs

	b.s. (before school)		a.s. (after school)	
	ACTIVITY	AUDITIONEES	ACTIVITY	AUDITIONEES
MON	Dance training	Rosie	Singing (learn words)	Rosie Soph Abs

TUES	Watch Banana Splits videos for tips & inspiration	Rosie	Dancing (practise routine)	Rosie Soph Abs
WEDS	Microphone technique (holding, singing into and dancing around)	Rosie	Singing (vocal exercises and staying in tune)	Rosie Soph Abs (extra homework)
THURS	Singing practice	Rosie	Acting class (how to really **perform** the song)	Rosie Soph Abs
FRI	Warm-ups and stretching exercises	Rosie	Costume-fitting	Rosie Soph Abs
SAT	All day dance rehearsals, followed by Banana Splits show in evening for performance tips and inspiration			
SUN	All day singing rehearsals			

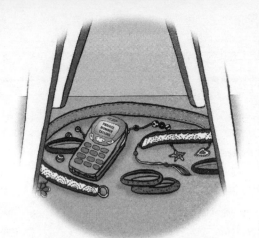

Chapter Three

One of the things I love most about Soph is that she's a total fashion genius. She's so good at customising stuff, she could even make some of Nan's outfits look cool. While Nan's fashion motto is 'what would Jessica Fletcher wear?' (Jessica Fletcher being her TV murder-mystery heroine), Soph's is 'pass me the scissors'.

'Wow,' said Frankie Gabriel, backstage at the *Pulse* auditions. 'Did you make those, Soph?'

We were wearing these amazing wraparound halter-tops, dyed jeans and Soph-original belts with all kinds of cool beads and charms hanging off them.

'Yep,' said Soph, with a grin.

'Seriously cool,' said Frankie, wandering off.

'Yay! I rock,' said Soph, happily.

Frankie's sister is this mega-famous super-model, so if anyone knows about fashion, it's her.

'You rock at designing stuff,' said Abs, 'but not at singing, right?'

'I know, I know,' said Soph. 'I mime the verses, then join in with the shouty "Jump!" bits in the chorus.'

'Exactly,' said me and Abs together. Soph has a famously terrible voice.

'OK, people,' shouted Time Lord. 'It's show time.'

I kid you not.

'Mr Falconer's here and we're ready to start. We want you to perform as you're called, individually or in your groups. Everyone happy?'

There were a few nods and Amanda Suck-up Hawkins simpered, 'Yes, sir.'

'Let's get this show on the road, then.'

'Could he *be* any cheesier?' said Abs, as Time Lord went and sat with Jim Falconer.

Me and Soph giggled, but nervously. The first group walked on to the stage. Suddenly, auditioning for an actual film director seemed like a much bigger deal than it had a few minutes earlier.

'Let's watch,' I said, and the three of us tiptoed over to the edge of the stage.

The first group was really good. Then Becky Blakeney from our year sang a solo, and she was brilliant, too. Lara Neils and Keira Roberts went out next and howled their way through 'Get The Party Started'. I laughed so hard, I almost didn't feel my mobile vibrating in my pocket, telling me I had a message.

'It's from Mum,' I whispered.

Don't forget – eyes & teeth. Break a leg!
:-D

'Eyes and teeth?' whispered Soph.

'Cheesy grin,' I told her. It's very sad I know,

but that's what you get when you live with someone who thinks learning dance routines is more important than cooking dinner.

'Hey,' said Abs, nudging me. 'It's Beyoncé Hawkins.'

Amanda had just stalked on stage and was busy flicking her hair as the backing music started.

'What's she singing?' I said.

'It's from *The Sound of Music*,' whispered Abs. 'My gran makes me watch it every Christmas. Time Lord must have picked it.'

Amanda began warbling in an opera-ish voice.

Me, Abs and Soph swapped a smug look, and I felt humongously glad we'd gone with Mum's song suggestion. As Amanda finished, Time Lord stood in front of the stage giving her a one-person standing ovation.

Amanda bowed and smiled in a very annoying way as he shouted, 'Bravo!'

'Good luck, losers,' she sneered, pushing past us. 'If your singing's as bad as those fashion-freak outfits, you'll need it.'

'Rosie Parker, Sophie McCoy, Abigail Flynn,' called Time Lord.

'Come on,' hissed Abs. She pulled me away from Amanda, and we followed Soph on to the stage.

'Hi,' said Mr Falconer. 'You're singing "Jump", right? Let's hear it.'

Time Lord aimed a remote control at the CD player and our music started.

For the first minute or so, it went brilliantly. My nerves more or less disappeared as soon as me and Abs started singing, and Soph remembered to mime until we got to the chorus.

'Jump!' the three of us sang, jumping up in the air, then turning round. We knew Mum's dance routine inside out after all that rehearsing.

'Jump!' we sang again, but as I landed, I suddenly felt something whizz past my ear. A bit of Soph's belt had flown off. Halfway through the second verse, Abs trod on it and over-balanced. She grabbed my arm and one of the bracelets I was wearing snapped. Soph was looking a bit panicky. There were beads everywhere. As we launched back into the chorus, I noticed one of the jewels Soph had stuck to Abs's jeans was starting to peel off too.

It was a massive relief when we eventually reached the end of the song.

'Great,' grinned Mr Falconer, clapping. 'That was terrific.'

Time Lord smiled too, although not quite as enthusiastically.

'We're announcing our decision tomorrow,' said Mr F. 'But you girls did a great job. Thanks.'

'Can we have Frankie Gabriel and Ella Gregory next?' called Time Lord.

We made our way off the stage as Frankie and Ella picked their way through bits of broken costume.

✳ ✳ ✳

Soph spent the next twenty minutes apologising, while me and Abs reassured her. I was pretty sure it hadn't made any difference and the rest of our performance had gone brilliantly. I sent Mum a text to let her know we'd eyed-and-teethed our socks off. Before we knew it, Time Lord came backstage to tell everyone the auditions were over.

'We had some excellent performances,' he said, nodding towards Amanda Hawkins, 'and even those without as much – ahem – *natural talent* tried their best, so well done everyone.'

There was a feeble round of applause before everyone started drifting off.

'Where's Soph?' I asked Abs, looking round.

Abs shrugged. 'She was here a minute ago.'

Most people were heading for the doors, so me and Abs had to shove our way back to the stage. We found Soph on her hands and knees in the wings.

'Er, Soph?' I said.

She looked up. 'The beads,' she said. 'I can totally fix the belts. I just need to find all the bits.'

With everyone who'd performed after us kicking them about, they'd scattered everywhere. There were a few broken ones, but plenty of them were fine. Me and Abs knelt down to help pick them up.

By the time we finished, everyone – including Time Lord and Mr Falconer – had left. Soph stuffed her last handful into a plastic bag we'd found backstage.

'Thanks,' she said, 'and I really am –'

'Sorry!' me and Abs finished. 'We know!'

'Zut alors,' I said as a phone rang nearby. 'I bet that's my mum again, asking if we know who got the parts.'

'I thought yours was on vibrate,' said Abs.

'Oh, yeah.'

We stood and listened for a minute.

'It's coming from over there,' said Soph, pointing.

We peered down from the stage. The ringing phone was on the floor under a chair, near where Time Lord and Jim Falconer had been sitting. I jumped down and picked it up.

'Don't answer it!' said Abs.

'It'll probably go to voicemail in a minute,' said Soph.

I hesitated, then pressed 'accept'. It was my chance to get some insider info on the film.

'It's all arranged for the twenty-fourth, Falconer,' said a gruff voice. 'Watch your back.'

And then it went dead.

I stared at the phone.

'What?' said Abs. 'Who was it?'

'Rosie Parker,' shouted a voice from the back of the hall, and all three of us jumped. It was Time Lord.

He came striding towards us, looking furious.

'You'd better have a very good explanation for this, young lady.'

'But –' I tried to say.

He snatched the phone.

'I don't want to hear it,' he ranted as the three of us stared at him. 'I know for a fact this doesn't belong to you, and you were about to steal it.'

'She wasn't,' Soph said.

'It was ringing and she answered it – that's all,' said Abs.

'I know I shouldn't have, but I thought it might be important,' I said, 'and it was. It sounds like someone's got it in for Mr Falconer.'

'Enough!' spat Time Lord. 'You were caught red-handed, and I've a good mind to tell Mr Falconer.'

'Tell Mr Falconer what, exactly?'

The four of us spun round again, this time to see the director coming back into the hall.

Time Lord opened and closed his mouth silently in a goldfishy sort of way.

'I – they –' he croaked. 'It wasn't me,' he eventually spluttered.

Mr Falconer gave him a really weird look. Time Lord held the phone out, and Mr F grabbed it, still staring. He turned round and stalked towards the door without saying anything.

'Jim,' Time Lord called after him. 'Surely you don't think *I* was trying to steal it . . .'

Mr F disappeared through the double doors. Time Lord turned on me, Abs and Soph. He had angry pink patches on his cheeks.

'Detention,' he said. 'Back here after lessons. And you're lucky I'm not sending you to the headmistress.'

He'd calmed down a bit by the time we turned up for detention.

'Right, ladies,' he said. 'The props cupboard needs clearing out. It shouldn't take more than half an hour.'

Soph rolled up her sleeves and Abs glared at me. I did feel bad. If I'd just ignored the phone, like they'd said, we'd all be on our way home. It felt seriously unfair, though. I really hadn't meant to do anything wrong.

'Mr Lord,' I said. 'This has nothing to do with Abs or Soph. It was me who answered the phone.'

He held up a hand. 'Let's just forget about it, shall we?'

'But sir, I really think Mr Falconer might be in trouble. The bloke on the other end sounded totally threatening – like a gangster or something.'

Time Lord laughed. 'Really, Rosie. You and your imagination.'

'I didn't imagine it,' I protested.

'She did look really scared,' added Soph.

'That's not the point,' said Time Lord. 'The three of you need to learn to respect other people's property. You had no right to be doing anything with that phone.'

Sulking, I gave up and he walked away.

'Thanks for sticking up for us,' said Abs.

I shrugged. 'I'm sorry I got us all into trouble.'

'Hey, at least we didn't lose our chance to be in the film,' Abs said.

'I hadn't thought of that,' said Soph. 'It would have been très awful after all those rehearsals.'

They carried on talking as we tidied the cupboard, but I wasn't really paying attention. Whatever Time Lord said, I hadn't imagined the voice on the end of the phone. 'Watch your back' was hardly something you'd say to a friend. And then there was the weird way Jim Falconer had reacted. There was definitely something fishy going on, and I was determined to find out what it was.

Chapter Four

We did it! Me, Abs and Soph were officially
going to be film stars. Time Lord posted the
list outside the drama studio. Frankie Gabriel
and Ella Gregory got through, too, and so did
Becky Blakeney. Not at all surprisingly, there
was no sign of Lara Neils or Keira Roberts on
the list, but Amanda Hawkins was right at the
top.

'What does "Oona" mean?' said Frankie,
reading the word next to Amanda's name on the
list. Hers, like mine, Abs's and Soph's, had the

words 'walk-on' alongside it. Amanda was the only one who had anything different.

'Duh,' said Amanda. 'It's a name.'

'Exactly,' said Time Lord, who was standing behind us. 'Those assigned as walk-ons will be extras in the background of each scene. Amanda is one of the talented few who'll be playing an actual character.'

'I get a line and everything,' Amanda boasted.

'Oona is a pivotal role in one of the film's early scenes,' Time Lord explained. 'Flick, Estelle Mayor's character, struggles with her studies, and Oona offers to help out. She's a gifted, hard-working student. Just like Amanda, in fact,' he added.

'Pass me the sick bucket,' I whispered.

Soph giggled.

'Hang on a minute,' said Abs. 'When Mr Falconer told us about the film, he mentioned something about that. Doesn't Flick get caught copying the class geek's homework?'

'Yeah,' I suddenly remembered. 'But then she realises it's the wrong thing to do and there's a song-and-dance routine about why cheating is bad.'

'What's that got to do with anything?' said Soph.

'Oona,' said Abs, with an evil grin, 'is the class geek. Amanda's playing a nerd!'

We all turned to look at Amanda, whose face had gone a very hilarious shade of pink.

'At least I'm not some no-name extra,' she said angrily. She stuck her nose in the air and pushed Frankie Gabriel out of the way so she could do her famous stalking-off-down-the-corridor bit.

'Amanda,' Time Lord called after her. 'I need to discuss your costume. Oona's spectacles are very thick and Mr Falconer needs to make sure you can see through them, because if you can't, he'll have to get them adjusted.'

He trotted after her and the rest of us burst out laughing. Amanda Hawkins playing a speccy geek? Seriously brilliantissimo.

* * *

As soon as we found out we were in the film, me, Abs and Soph were even keener than normal for term to end. Time Lord had handed out schedules and we were due to start work on the first day of the holidays.

'It's a small production, so we'll be helping the crew prepare for the first few days,' Time Lord explained. 'Filming proper starts on day three. That's when the lead actors will join us.'

Unbelievably, we still didn't have the first idea *who* the stars were.

'Bet you I find out by the time we go home,' I said to Abs and Soph, as Mum dropped us off on the first day of the holidays.

'They'll be here the day after tomorrow,' said Abs.

'I know,' I said. 'But it would be cool to find out who they are before everyone else does.'

'Do I look OK?' said Soph changing the subject. She was wearing a cute vintage mini-dress over a pair of capri pants. Me and Abs had gone for plain jeans and T-shirts.

'Just right,' said a voice behind us.

'Hi, Mr Falconer,' I said.

'Jim,' he said. 'Now we're working together, there'll be none of this "Mr" business. I'm Jim to everybody.' He grinned. 'Right, if you three are ready, I've got a trailer full of costumes that need moving from the car park into form-room C – otherwise known as our wardrobe department.'

Soph looked like she'd snuffed it and gone to fashion heaven. Getting a sneak peek at some of the costumes was pretty cool. We headed off to the trailer and started carrying armfuls of clothes into the school building. It took most of the morning to hang everything in order on metal racks. Then we helped the costume assistant put up screens to make a changing-room area.

After lunch in the catering van – the school canteen was part of Jim's film set – we helped set up the make-up room, the props department and finally some camera equipment. I didn't have a single second to try to find out who'd be starring in the film.

'I told you,' said Abs, in a very annoying way, as we headed home on the number 43 bus.

'I'll find out tomorrow,' I said, too tired even to argue.

* * *

'So, how was it?' Nan asked the second I got home.

'Cool,' I yawned.

'Tiring day, eh?'

'Yeah, but it was brilliant,' I said.

'Come and sit down while I make you something to eat,' said Nan.

She tottered off into the kitchen and I followed. I *was* pretty starving.

'There's a nice piece of ham and I'll boil a bit of broccoli and make us some of that pasty you're so fond of to go with it,' said Nan.

'It's *pasta*,' I giggled.

'Past*a*,' said Nan. 'It would've been potatoes or nothing in my day, but I'm not too old to move with the times.'

I sat at the kitchen table and watched her

bustling about, opening cupboards and drawers. Mum was out with one of her friends, so Nan was loving the chance to play head chef for once.

'There's a lovely *Miss Marple* on later,' she said, still bustling.

Oh, joy. People with bad hair getting done in, crying because their relatives have been done in or trying to cover up the fact they've done someone in. What could be more fun?

'Nan,' I said, suddenly remembering something, 'how can you tell if someone's really in trouble? I mean, say you answered a phone and the person at the other end said "watch your back", then hung up. That's not a good thing, right?'

She looked at me in a squinty-eyed kind of way.

'It depends,' she said, chopping some broccoli. 'It might just be friendly advice. Who're we talking about?'

I explained about Jim, and the phone call and the way he'd behaved.

'He seemed fine today,' I said, 'but I keep thinking about the phone call.'

Nan stopped chopping.

'The first rule of sleuthing,' she said, waggling the knife about in a très alarming way, 'is "never judge a book by its cover". This Jim person mightn't be in trouble at all. He could be the one who's up to no good.'

I thought for a second. 'No way. He's really nice. If he was up to something, he'd be –'

'Shifty?' Nan suggested.

'Yes. And he totally isn't. If I hadn't known about the phone weirdness, I'd never have guessed anything was up.'

'Well, maybe it was just a big misunderstanding,' said Nan. 'How much pasty do you want?'

* * *

When we arrived at school the next morning, the sports field was covered with giant metal crates. Time Lord, the crew and the other extras were hanging round. As we wandered over to join them, Jim appeared from inside the building.

'Morning, all,' he said. 'You've spotted my crates, then?'

'What are they for?' said Amanda.

'Are you thinking what I'm thinking?' whispered Abs.

I nodded. 'Pack her inside one and ship it somewhere they still have cannibals.'

The three of us cracked up.

'They're for furniture and equipment from inside the school,' Jim explained. 'I'm keeping a few bits and pieces, but mostly we're using our own props.'

'Why?' said Ella Gregory.

'Whitney High isn't exactly how I pictured the school in my film, so I'm changing things round a bit,' Jim said. 'Plus, we need extra room for the cameras to move about.'

'Wouldn't it have been easier to build a set?' said Abs.

'Definitely,' Jim grinned, 'but sets cost money. The great thing about Whitney High, apart from having you lot as extras, of course, is that it's free.'

'Remember, Jim's an independent filmmaker,' Time Lord chipped in.

Jim nodded. 'Directors working for big film companies can easily afford to build sets, but me . . .' He turned his pockets inside out to show they were empty. 'The crates cost next to nothing and we've borrowed most of the props, so it works out much cheaper.'

He looked around. 'OK, we need to get into groups and take one area each. I've drawn a plan of the school with everything marked on it. There are labels for the crates to make sure everything goes back where it came from.'

He handed round a pile of plans and labels.

'These are cool,' said Soph, studying the plan. 'He's drawn everything. All the desks and chairs . . . ooh, look. That's where we sit in French! That exact seat is mine. FR19.'

It really doesn't take much to make Soph happy.

We teamed up with Ella, Frankie Gabriel, Becky Blakeney and two blokes from the camera crew, because Abs said they would be good for lifting heavy stuff. As Soph had taken such an interest in the French classroom, that was the one we had to tackle. The plans were a cool way to organise everything, actually. Each room had its own code – FR for French room, LB for library, DS for drama studio, and so on – and then each thing in the room had a number. We wrote the numbers on stickers, slapped them on everything we moved, then added bigger stickers to the outsides of the crates so we'd know where to put everything after filming finished.

'I hadn't thought of that,' said Soph, dropping her end of the desk we were carrying.

'What?' said Abs, who was following behind us with two stacked chairs.

'Putting everything back again.'

I did my raising-one-eyebrow trick on her. 'Did you think we were going to have all next year's lessons in a crate, Soph?'

'No,' she protested. 'I just hadn't thought about it.'

'Oi, Fashion Freak. Move!'

Amanda Hawkins shoved Soph against the wall of the corridor and knocked our desk out of the way so she could get past.

'Here's an idea, lame-brain,' I snapped, 'try saying "excuse me" next time.'

'Or,' said Amanda, 'you losers could keep out of my way.'

'Is there a problem?' said Time Lord, who'd followed Amanda out of the library. They were each carrying one of the new computers we'd got at the start of last term. Like those were anywhere near as heavy as the desks and chairs we'd been lugging about.

'I was asking Rosie if she thought it was a good idea to leave that desk in the middle of the corridor,' Amanda simpered.

What's that I smell? Oh, yes, it's a lying troll.

'We were just moving it, sir,' said Soph, before Time Lord had chance to launch into one of his lectures.

'That would seem sensible,' he said, squeezing past us.

Amanda turned round and stuck her tongue out as they walked away.

I sooo couldn't wait to see her dressed as a geek.

Chapter Five

After a whole day of packing furniture into crates, I was seriously looking forward to a bit of celebness the following morning. I'd enjoyed myself so far, but it hadn't exactly been glamorous.

'It'll be so cool to see Estelle again,' said Soph, as the three of us made our way to the main hall, where the first scene was being shot.

'We'll finally get to see who the other stars are,' I said. 'I still can't believe –'

'– you didn't find out before?' said Abs. 'We know!'

'The first ever failure for super-sleuth Rosie Parker,' Soph mock-snivelled.

'Ha, ha,' I said, although I couldn't be properly huffy. I *had* been going on about it loads.

'That *is* it with the mystery stuff now, right?' Abs checked. 'You're about to find out who's in the film and that whole Jim's-phone thing didn't come to anything, so we can relax and get on with being film stars, can't we?'

'Maybe,' I said slowly. 'I mean, I can. I'm just not sure you two have got enough star quality.'

'Get her!' shouted Abs, and they chased me down the corridor. We flew through the hall doors, laughing like loons, and bumped straight into a tall, dark très handsome boy.

Cringe. *Cringe.* CRINGE.

'Hey,' he said, flashing a dangerously gorgeous grin. 'You're keen.'

'Rosie!' squealed a tiny girl with black hair who came dashing towards us. Estelle! She squashed me in a monster hug, then did the same to Abs and Soph.

'Leon,' she said, turning to the dark-haired boy, 'these are my friends, the girls I told you about. Rosie, Abs, Soph, this is Leon Harper.'

'Hi,' said Soph, swoonily.

'Nice to meet you,' said Abs, shaking his hand.

'I'm Rosie,' I said.

And then, just when you thought we were at maximum gorge-factor, another boy wandered over and slung his arm round Estelle's shoulder. He was blonde, with a toothpaste-advert smile.

'And this,' said Estelle, grinning up at him, 'is Harris.'

She introduced us to him.

'Hey dudes. Are you, like, in the film, too?' said Harris.

'We're extras,' I explained.

He looked at me blankly. 'Extra whats?'

'Extras,' Estelle told him. 'You know, the people in the background when we're acting. They'll be the other students in the school.'

He still looked confused. Estelle shook her head and carried on.

'I was so excited when Jim told me you'd be here,' she said. 'We've got loads to catch up on. There should be plenty of time to hang out between takes. Hey, Mia!' she shouted to another girl who'd just walked in. 'Come and meet my friends.'

We all said hello to Mia, who had curly red hair and amazingly blue eyes.

'I love your top,' she said to Soph, who beamed and explained she'd made it herself.

'No way,' said Mia. 'Could you make one for me?'

'Do the Swiss like cuckoo clocks?' I said.

Harris looked like his brain might melt from trying to work out the answer, and the rest of us started laughing.

'Uh-oh,' I said, stopping. I'd just spotted a horribly familiar figure coming towards us.

'Morning all,' said Time Lord, and then he noticed who we were talking to. 'Miss Mayor,' he said in an awed kind of voice.

Estelle seemed baffled. 'Hello,' she said, shaking the hand he'd held out to her.

'Estelle, this is our drama teacher, Time – Mr Lord,' I said.

'Tim, Tim. You must call me Tim,' babbled Time Lord. 'I'm an old friend of Jim's. We were at drama school together. Jim and Tim. Ha-ha-ha! I was – well, shouldn't blow my own trumpet, but I was a mentor figure to him. And now, of course, we've both gone on to bigger and better things. *Doctor Who* – I was a Cyberman – and now this. I'm playing Bob, the science teacher, but I'm sure Jim's already told you that.'

'Er . . .' said Estelle, who looked like she'd been slapped across the face with a wet kipper.

'Hi,' said Leon, grabbing Mr Lord's hand and shaking it. 'Leon. I'm playing Ben.'

Estelle smiled at him gratefully.

'Marvellous, wonderful, thrilled to meet you,' Time Lord squeaked.

It's hilariously tragic how over-excited he gets around celebrities.

Leon introduced him to Harris and Mia. Before you could say 'get a life, saddo', Time Lord had whipped out his battered old autograph book.

'Just a few new signatures for the collection,' he gabbled, pushing it first towards Estelle and then the others. There was an awkward silence as each of them signed. Harris took twice as long as the others and accidentally spelled his name with three Rs.

Luckily, Jim then called everyone together to start filming. The idea of trying to involve Time Lord in our conversation was too hideous to think about.

* * *

Unfortunately, over the next few weeks, we had to think about it and, in fact, put up with it quite a bit.

The filming turned out to be every bit as brilliant as me, Abs and Soph had hoped. With no mystery to solve, and no real work to do, we could relax between takes, unlike the last time we were on a movie set. All that stuff you read about making films being boring? Well, not if you're making a film with Estelle, Leon, Mia and Harris. The seven of us had the best time, chatting, listening to music and joking around. The only downside was Time Lord. He made a beeline for us whenever he wasn't filming, and with such a miniscule part, that was A LOT. It was like being at a party and having your embarrassing uncle turn up to do his balloon-animal tricks. In the end, we got really good at hiding.

The other person who tried mega-hard to mess things up was Amanda Hawkins. Shocking, I know. But for once, everything wasn't going her way.

Eight things to wipe the smug smile off Amanda Hawkins's face:

1. She has a totally obvious crush on Leon, but he can see straight through her annoyingly perfect face to her annoyingly annoying personality underneath.
2. Leon seems to have a bit of a thing for Abs.

They're seriously cute together – always hanging out, sharing silly jokes. Amanda can't stand Abs, so this winds her up a hilarious amount.

3. Even though Time Lord is always going on about how brilliant she is, Jim clearly doesn't agree. She's trying sooo hard to suck up to him, but it's not working.

4. Her geek costume is très horrible: a grey school shirt, this gross skirt with a lumpy waistband, wrinkly tights, a hairband that even my mum would think was a bit old-fashioned and, of course, the chunky specs.

5. The glasses are so thick she keeps bumping into stuff. Jim says clumsiness is great for her character, so she has to wear them.

6. Her one line is: 'I could help you if you like', but every time Jim shouts 'action', she says, 'I could like you if you help'. EVERY TIME!

7. Instead of acting like a normal person in front of the camera, she does this thing where her arms and legs go stiff like sticks. I

suspect the next person who says to her 'just act naturally' will get a duffing-up.

8. Without Lara and Keira around, she is forced to hang out with Time Lord. This cannot be a good thing.

One afternoon, a few weeks after filming started, I was joking around by the catering van with Mia, Estelle, Harris and Leon. Abs had left early to babysit her little sister, and Soph had gone to get started on some jeans she was customising for Mia. The five of us were eating chips and laughing about the way Jim had to keep yelling 'cut!' during Time Lord's scenes, because his hair had gone bonkers again.

'The make-up girl must've used a year's supply of gel on him,' Estelle giggled.

'It's like his hair just slurps it up,' said Mia.

'I think superglue is the answer,' I said.

'Or,' suggested Leon, 'a bobble hat.'

'Er, Harris?' said Estelle. He'd suddenly started waving, which seemed a bit random, even for him.

'What are you doing?'

'Waving,' said Harris.

'Yeah, we get that,' said Estelle, raising her eyebrows. '*Why* are you waving?'

'Because *she's* waving at me,' said Harris, pointing.

As I turned to look, my stomach did a horrible back-flip. There, walking across the car park, was my mum. Like Harris had said, she was waving.

'Sacrebleu,' I said, faintly.

The others looked at me. 'My mum,' I mumbled. She was half an hour early to pick me up, and it sooo obviously wasn't an accident. She'd been dropping hints for days about feeling left out and how we wouldn't even be in the film if it wasn't for her.

'Yoo-hoo,' shouted Mum, beaming as she came towards us.

'Hi, Mum,' I said dully. As I didn't have much choice, I introduced her to the others.

'Lovely to meet you,' said Mum, as they all shook her hand. 'I've heard a lot about you.'

WHY? Why do parents ALWAYS have to say

that? I *swear* they're embarrassing on purpose.

'So how's the filming going?' said Mum.

I tried to send her a telepathic message. *You are not hanging out with me and my mates.*

'Great,' said Estelle. 'Really good.'

And then, with genius timing for once, Time Lord appeared and saved my bacon.

'Sorry to interrupt,' he said. 'Jim needs Estelle and Leon on set. We've got to re-shoot the library scene. Some sort of problem with my hair, apparently.'

'Hi,' said Mum. 'It's Mr Lord, isn't it? We met at parents' evening. I'm Rosie's mum.'

'Of course,' nodded Time Lord. 'Good to see you again.'

He looked at his watch.

'Nice to meet you, Mrs Parker,' said Leon.

'Bye,' said Estelle.

'Barbecue!' said Mum in a way-too-loud voice as they walked away.

'Sorry?' said Time Lord.

'We're having a barbecue,' Mum said. 'Next

Sunday. I know you don't work on Sundays, so I thought you might all like to come along. About three-ish? Rosie's got the address. Of course she has – she lives there. Ha-ha-ha!'

Oh, good grief.

* * *

As soon as we got home, I instant-messaged Abs and Soph. This was a massivo emergency.

NosyParker: Nightmare! Mum's invited everyone round for a barbecue.

CutiePie: Everyone who?

NosyParker: Estelle, Mia, Harris, Leon and Time Lord.

FashionPolice: Zut alors!

CutiePie: Are they coming?

NosyParker: Yep. I think they were too stunned to say no.

CutiePie: So Leon's coming?

FashionPolice: You lurve him.

NosyParker: Hel-lo? This is une problemo enormioso. If anyone at school finds out Time Lord has been to my house, I won't be able to stand the shame.

CutiePie: But if they find out you had four film stars round for dinner, they'll think you rock.

NosyParker: I suppose.

FashionPolice: It's like maths. Four celebs cancel out one teacher.

CutiePie: Yeah, Soph. It's EXACTLY like maths. Did they definitely all say they were coming?

NosyParker: YES. Including Time Lord. What am I going to do?

FashionPolice: Buy a new outfit.

CutiePie: Chill out. It'll be fab.

NosyParker: You think?

CutiePie: Bien sûr, ma soeur.

I still wasn't convinced. I seriously hoped Soph was right and Abs wasn't just keen to hang out with Leon. If Amanda Hawkins ever found out Time Lord had been at my house, I'd be toast.

Chapter Six

BARBECUE MENU

Bowls of olives (with suspicious, greenish-coloured,
home-made marinade)

Bowls of peanuts (out of a packet, so probably taste OK)

Salad with dressing (i.e. vinegar)

French bread (très crusty)

Garlic bread (with giant lumps of garlic that make your breath
smell like vampire repellent)

Sausages (burnt or raw)

Chicken (pink in the middle, possibly deadly)

Trifle (Nan's contribution, probably contains dust
and chunks of custard cream)

Once everyone arrived, I had to admit it was an OK idea. Who wouldn't be excited about having a garden full of film stars?

'It's like a dream come true,' sighed Soph, who was especially happy because Mia was wearing the jeans she'd designed.

'Having fun?' called Mum, dancing past on her way to the kitchen.

As well as going a bit nuts on the food side, she'd made about twenty CDs filled with dodgy eighties music. The stereo had been blaring all afternoon.

'Yes!' I shouted and she gave me a thumbs-up.

'This is brilliant,' sighed Estelle, lying back in one of our garden chairs. 'It's so nice just to chill out.'

'Aren't you enjoying making the film?' asked Abs. She was sitting next to Leon and had hardly stopped grinning since he'd arrived.

'I love it,' said Estelle. 'I just haven't had many days off since I won *Stage-Struck*.'

'Well, as I've always said, the business is tougher than people realise,' said Time Lord, sitting down next to us. He was wearing jeans with a crease ironed down the front of each leg and a totally tragic T-shirt that said 'Doctor Who Went to the End of the Universe and All I Got Was this Lousy T-Shirt'. As if the 'My Other Car Is a Tardis' sticker he's got on the back of his teachermobile isn't sad enough.

'Long hours are the norm, and days off are a luxury for most actors,' he droned. But just as I was trying to work out how to avoid another of his yawn-a-rama lectures, Mum reappeared.

'Ooh, I love this song,' she said, putting a tray of drinks down on the table.

'Me too,' nodded Time Lord. 'They don't make them like this any more.'

'That's what I'm always saying!' Mum beamed.

'Fancy a bop?' said Time Lord.

I bit the inside of my cheeks to stop myself laughing out loud.

The two of them shimmied off into the middle of the garden and started dancing in a mucho hilarioso fashion.

'Is he always like this?' giggled Estelle.

'Yep,' said me, Soph and Abs all together.

'Wouldn't it be funny if he got together with your mum?' said Leon.

'Shut *up*!' I howled. 'That's sooo not happening. Unfunny Brian was bad enough.'

'Who?' said Mia, and I launched into a whole explanation of Mum's ex-boyfriend and his un-hilariousness.

'I know how you feel,' said Estelle. 'My mum once dated a bank manager who dressed up like a Viking at the weekends.'

As we carried on swapping stories about rubbish parents, I noticed Harris had been cornered by Nan. Even though I love her a lot, she is a bit bonkers, and I was pretty sure Harris wouldn't have a clue what she was going on about. I tuned my ears out of the parents convo and started listening to Nan and Harris. (This is a très useful skill for people like me who want to be journalists, as well as excellent for general nosiness purposes.)

'So, this Jim chap,' Nan was saying. 'What's he like to work with?'

'He's kind of tall, he wears this scarf thingy quite a lot and he's always eating mints,' said Harris.

'Mince?' said Nan.

'Yeah, the ones in the green packets,' said Harris.

'But what's he *like*?' Nan said. 'Is he a cheerful sort, or does he shout a lot?'

'He sometimes shouts,' said Harris. 'It's really noisy when everyone's singing at the same time. We can't hear what he's saying unless he shouts.'

There was silence for a minute. I guessed Nan was trying to work out what Miss Marple or Inspector Morse's next line of enquiry would be.

'Have you noticed him doing anything suspicious?' she finally said.

'I don't think so,' said Harris

'What about any odd phone calls?'

'Oh, yeah,' said Harris. 'I had one the other day. My friend Boomer rang up and pretended to be that bloke off *Who Wants to Be a Millionaire?* It was brilliant.'

Nan sighed. 'You wouldn't say there was anything fishy about him, then. You don't think this Jim person could be involved in something shady?'

'You're talking about *Jim?*' said Leon, and I jumped. I hadn't realised the others were listening to Nan's conversation, too.

'Jim Falconer?' laughed Leon.

Mia and Estelle were giggling.

'Where on earth did you get that idea?'

'From Rosie,' said Nan.

They all stared at me.

'It was nothing,' I said, cringing. 'I answered Jim's phone a few weeks ago and there was this weird-sounding bloke on the other end, that's all.'

'Blackmail, it sounded like,' said Nan. 'Rosie thought Jim was in danger, but I'm not sure he isn't up to something dastardly.'

Dastardly? I ask you.

'Jim's cool,' Estelle assured her. 'We haven't seen anything even vaguely strange going on.'

'What did the person on the phone say?' Leon asked me.

'"Watch your back",' I said.

'Maybe it was his doctor,' he said. 'Have you seen the way Jim dances? Totally bound to put his back out sooner or later.'

Everyone except me and Nan started laughing again. I felt my cheeks going beetrooty. Seriously, what is wrong with me? I think all the murder-mystery shows I'm forced to watch with Nan have sent my mystery radar round the bend. I have to stop finding mysteries everywhere. Oh, and stop talking to Nan, too.

'Earth to Rosie,' said Abs.

'What?'

'You haven't noticed, have you?' she said.

I followed the direction of her gaze, and groaned. Mum and Time Lord had just started dancing to 'Jump'.

* * *

The following afternoon, we were all back on set and really excited about the scene we were filming next. It was the bit in the movie where Flick (Estelle's character), Tula (Mia), Richie (Harris) and Jake (Leon) get ready for the big school dance in the main hall. All the extras, including me, Soph and Abs, join in with this coolissimo dance, and at the end, everyone dances out into the corridors. It took the crew ages to set everything up. When we were eventually ready to start, no one could find Jim.

'OK,' yelled the assistant director, 'I can't get through to his mobile. I want everyone to split up and check the building. We haven't got all afternoon, so be back here in ten minutes.

Someone's bound to have found him by then.'

We'd spent most of the morning sitting in wardrobe and make-up, so it was cool to have something to do. We all dashed off in different directions. I decided to head towards the science block. Exactly what I thought Jim would be doing hanging around Bunsen-burner HQ, I didn't know, but no one else was going in that direction. There was no sign of him when I got there, and it was time to head back. As I came out of the lab, I suddenly spotted someone out on the sports field. It was Jim. He was pacing up and down near the crates, tapping a text message into his mobile phone. He kept texting for a minute, then slipped the phone into his pocket.

'Jim!' I yelled, and he looked up. A second later, he bounded over.

'Blimey,' he said. 'Lost track of time. Is everyone ready?'

'Yep.'

'Great,' he said, smiling weakly. 'Thanks.'

And we walked back to the hall.

It took the rest of the afternoon to film the big dance scene. We were all exhausted by the time Jim shouted 'cut' for the last time.

'That's a wrap for today,' he announced. 'Great work, everyone. I'll see you back here in the morning. One more thing,' he added, raising his voice over the noise in the hall, 'I've lost my mobile. If any of you spot it on your way out, I'd be grateful if you could get it back to me.'

He turned round and started chatting to Time Lord, who was hovering about ten centimetres behind Jim as usual. Seriously, he's such a suck-up. Everyone else made their way out of the hall and I followed Abs and Soph, my mystery radar well and truly spinning. I couldn't ignore the fact that this was totally suspicious. I'd definitely seen Jim put the phone in his pocket out on the playing field. How could he have lost it since then? Maybe Nan was right for once. Maybe Jim *was* up to something dodgy. Why would he lie about losing his phone?

Chapter Seven

'You're quiet,' said Abs, as the three of us got changed. 'What's up?'

'I'll tell you later,' I said. Amanda Hawkins was on the other side of the changing rooms and I couldn't risk her overhearing. She has a mouth like a megaphone when it comes to spreading gossip and rumours.

We finished getting dressed and headed out into the corridor. Jim was walking a little way ahead of us, talking to Leon and Estelle, with Time Lord trailing behind. We'd found out at the party that Jim was staying at Time Lord's house, which explained why he was looking more and more irritated. Being around Time Lord at home *and* at work would do anyone's head in.

'Another day's filming in the can, eh girls?' said Time Lord, catching sight of us.

'I loved doing that scene,' said Estelle.

'Me too,' nodded Soph.

'Your dancing was great,' said Leon, looking straight at Abs, who went pink.

'It all looked terrific on camera,' said Jim.

'Have you found your phone yet?' Abs asked him.

Jim shook his head.

'Hang on,' I said, in a genius bit of improvising. 'My trainer's come undone.' I stopped walking and so did Abs and Soph. 'We'll catch up with you,' I said to Estelle and the others.

They carried on walking as I pretended to re-tie my shoe.

'OK, spill,' said Abs, when I stood up again. 'What's going on?'

'Ssssh,' I hissed, pulling them to one side. The

corridor was more or less deserted, but as Nan is forever telling me, walls have ears. It means 'keep your voice down', although I don't know why she can't just say that.

Whispering, I filled them in on Jim and his phone and the weirdness of him lying about it.

'I don't know,' said Abs when I'd finished. 'It does sound –' She broke off as a phone started ringing somewhere close by.

'Exactly like that,' I said. If it wasn't Jim's phone, it was one with an identical ringtone.

'It's coming from that,' said Soph, pointing at a radiator.

All three of us peered behind it, and saw the phone's screen flashing as it rang. I slid my arm down to try and reach it.

'Be careful,' said Abs.

'Yeah,' nodded Soph. 'If you get your arm stuck, they'll have to come and cut you out. I've seen it on TV, and they always cut through your clothes as well. I'd be gutted for you if that top got wrecked.'

'Thanks for that, Soph.' I pulled my arm out

and held the phone up triumphantly. 'It's Jim's. I *knew* he hadn't really lost it.'

'If Time Lord finds us with it again, we'll be in detention for the rest of our lives,' Abs hissed, looking nervously along the corridor.

She had a point.

'In here,' I said, grabbing her and Soph and pulling them into the girls' toilets.

'I don't get it,' said Soph. 'We're giving the phone back to him, aren't we?'

'Yes,' I said, 'but first of all we're going to find out who he texted this afternoon, and see if there's any more suspicious stuff on it.'

'Says who?' Abs argued. 'You can't just snoop into people's private business.'

'How else are we going to find out what's going on?' I said. 'Either Jim's in trouble, or he's up to something, and we can't do anything until we know which one it is. This —' I waggled the phone about '— is the answer.'

'Fine,' said Abs. She took the phone and flipped it open.

'Dialled numbers,' I said, as she scrolled through the menu. She pressed the 'select' key and a list of numbers appeared.

'They're not much use,' said Soph. 'We don't know who they belong to.'

'If the people he was calling were in his address book, those would be names instead of numbers,' said Abs. 'My dad's got the same phone.'

'So, he's calling people he doesn't know very well,' I said, thoughtfully.

'And Time Lord,' said Soph. Abs had just found 'Tim Lord'.

'Check the "sent messages" folder,' I suggested and Abs got clicking.

'That's it!' I said, pointing. 'That one. Two o'clock this afternoon was just after we left the hall to look for him.'

'It's just numbers again,' said Soph, as Abs opened the message. 'Doesn't he know you can use letters on these things?'

I peered at the screen. Instead of an actual message, there was just a list of what looked like code numbers. They seemed kind of familiar.

'There are numbers *and* letters,' said Abs.

'The crates!' we both said, recognising what the list meant at the same time.

Soph looked at the message again.

'Oh, yeah,' she said. 'The labels we put on the crates when we packed everything.'

'That was where Jim was when I saw him texting,' I said. 'Out on the sports field, right by the crates.'

'But why would he be sending the numbers to someone?' said Abs.

'I don't know,' I said, biting my lip and thinking hard. 'But if we find out which crates the numbers belong to and what's in them, I bet we'll be able to work out what Jim's up to.'

'Yeah,' Soph said. 'If we had the list, we could match them up.'

'But he collected the lists after we finished the packing,' said Abs.

'I think you two are forgetting something, apart from how to use your brains properly,' I said. 'We don't need the list of numbers – we can go outside and look at the stickers on the crates.'

'Oh, yeah,' said Soph again.

I checked my watch. 'The caretaker locks up at half past. We should be able to make it to the crates, check the numbers, and get out before he shuts the main gates.'

'I really can't,' said Abs. 'I'm already late. I've got to babysit again, and Mum'll ground me for the rest of the summer if I'm not home on time.'

'OK,' I said. 'Me and Soph'll check the crates and let you know what we find out.'

She handed me the phone and pushed the toilet door open.

'Good luck,' she whispered.

'Roger that,' I said, saluting. 'Over and out.'

CutiePie: Are you home yet?

NosyParker: Yup. You, Soph?

FashionPolice: Oui, oui, mes amis.

CutiePie: So, what's the story, Rory?

NosyParker: The numbers all match the LB crates.

CutiePie: LB was the stuff from the library, wasn't it? The things Amanda and Time Lord's team packed.

NosyParker: Exactamundo. And what did we see them carrying?

CutiePie: Zut alors! The computer equipment.

FashionPolice: The mega-expensive, brand-new, so-much-of-it-there's-hardly-room-for-any-books-in-the-library computer equipment.

NosyParker: Have you been drinking that funny orange squash again, Soph?

FashionPolice: I'm just saying the stuff in those crates is worth loads of money.

CutiePie: So what the crusty old grandads is going on?

NosyParker: Stealing?

CutiePie: Jim stealing the computer equipment, you mean?

NosyParker: I don't know. It sounds horrible. But maybe Nan was right about him being shifty.

CutiePie: Remember when he told us why he was using the crates instead of building a set?

NosyParker: Yep. Empty pockets.

FashionPolice: So we know he's a bit short of money.

CutiePie: It does sound seriously dodgy.

FashionPolice: What can we do, though?

NosyParker: I'm not sure.

FashionPolice: We could ask Rosie's Nan.

NosyParker: Au contraire, mes frères. I am officially not telling her about mystery stuff any more.

CutiePie: It's probably too late to do anything now. Let's wait until tomorrow.

FashionPolice: What should I wear?

Chapter Eight

It felt weird going back to Whitney High the next morning. Luckily, we weren't in any scenes until later in the day, so we didn't have to spend much time with Jim. I had his phone in my bag. Even though I was trying hard to look normal and innocent, I felt like there was a giant sign above my head saying 'phone stealer'.

'The thing is,' I told Abs and Soph, 'if Jim *is* planning to steal the computer equipment, losing his phone might be like an alibi.'

The three of us were watching them film the

scene where Flick (Estelle), who's going out with Richie (Harris), realises she's actually in love with Jake (Leon), and Tula (Mia), who's going out with Jake, realises she's in love with Richie.

'How d'you mean?' said Soph.

'Well, if the computers get stolen, the police question everyone, right? Jim tells them he lost his phone. When it's found, the police check his messages and see the one with the crate numbers in the sent folder, but they'll know Jim didn't send it because he'd lost the phone. They'll think someone else stole the phone, sent the numbers and then dumped it.'

'And everyone on set can say it's true, because he announced it at the end of filming yesterday,' said Abs.

'He's good,' said Soph.

'Quiet, please,' called Jim from the other side of the room. 'We're going for a take.'

We sat and watched as Estelle and the others had a very confusing conversation about who loved who and why. It was the third time we'd watched them run through it, and I was getting a headache. As the cameras rolled, I glanced over at Jim. He seemed jumpy and kept looking out of the window towards the sports field.

When the scene finished, there was an awkward pause.

'Oh . . . yes, um, cut!' Jim eventually managed.

'Talk about distracted,' Abs muttered, while the crew re-set everything for another take.

'He keeps looking at the crates,' I said.

Abs and Soph nodded.

'Nothing could happen in daylight, could it?' said Soph. 'Not with so many people here.'

'No,' said Abs. 'He'd have to be barking to think he could get away with it.'

'Abs,' I said. Something was clicking into place in my brain. 'What's the date?'

'The twenty-fourth. Remember – it's our last proper day of filming.'

'Aw, sad,' said Soph.

'"It's all arranged for the twenty-fourth",' I said.

'What?'

'That was what the dodgy-sounding man said when I answered Jim's phone,' I told them. '"It's all arranged for the twenty-fourth, Falconer. Watch your back.".'

'He didn't say the twenty-fourth of when, though,' pointed out Soph.

'It was over a month ago,' said Abs. 'This is the second twenty-fourth since the end of term.'

'And we don't know that phone call had anything to do with this,' added Soph.

'But it *could* be today,' I argued. 'We can't wait around to find out – we need to talk to Jim.'

'Confront him, you mean?' said Soph.

'Exactly.'

'There's just one teeny-tiny problem,' said Abs, who I could tell was about to go into super-sensible mode. 'If Jim and whoever he's working with are up for stealing computers from a school, they're probably prepared to do the odd bit of kidnapping or torture, or at least some serious duffing-up.'

'You mean they're dangerous?' said Soph.

'Well, duh,' said Abs. 'It just doesn't seem very likely they'll let three fourteen-year-old girls stop them.'

'But what else can we do?' I said.

'Time Lord,' Abs suggested.

'Time Lord?' I said. 'You *are* joking?'

'No,' said Abs, huffily. 'I know he's not the kind of person you'd normally go to with a problem, but he knows us, and he knows Jim, and the evidence is pretty convincing.'

'It's not a bad idea,' said Soph.

'What's not a bad idea?' asked Estelle.

The three of us looked up. We hadn't even noticed the others approaching.

'They're going to be a while re-setting,' said Mia, indicating the camera crew. 'What's up?'

I looked at Abs and Soph in a 'what d'you think?' kind of way.

'If we tell them, they might be able to help,' said Abs.

* * *

A few minutes later, Estelle, Harris, Leon and Mia looked as horrified as we felt. Actually, Harris looked confused, but the others were all totally shocked.

'I'm sorry we didn't believe you the other day,' said Estelle. 'I feel awful.'

'It's just so hard to imagine Jim doing anything dodgy,' said Mia.

'He's the man,' said Harris.

'Now I think about it,' said Leon, 'he was always on the phone arguing about money and loans and investors at the start of filming. Remember those scenes we did at his friend's house in London?' he said to the others.

'It was meant to be Flick's house,' Mia explained. 'All our characters hang out in her bedroom at the start of the film. Tula and Flick have this sleepover one night as well.'

'Yeah,' said Leon. 'Jim seemed anxious all the time when we were filming there. But by the time we arrived on set here, I thought he'd sorted it. He found this place, the crew's been paid, we've got props and costumes – everything's gone so smoothly, I just assumed he'd found the money.'

'What if he just borrowed it?' Abs said. 'He might still be desperate for the cash.'

'We can't just sit here and do nothing,' I said.

'We should go to Time Lord,' said Abs again.

'Good idea,' nodded Leon. 'He's a pain, but I bet he'd know what to do.'

'Will you come with us?' said Abs. 'What you overheard is extra evidence. It makes it seem more . . . convincing.'

'What Abs means,' I said, 'is Time Lord's more likely to believe you than us.'

'We were all mushrooms in our last school play,' said Soph. 'He doesn't exactly think we're brilliant.'

'No problemo,' grinned Leon.

'We'll all come with you, if you think it'll help,' said Estelle.

Mia and Harris nodded.

'Cool,' said Abs. 'All we've got to do is find Time Lord, and make sure Jim isn't around.'

* * *

We snatched our chance half an hour later. We'd moved on to the canteen to film the next scene. The crew was setting up, ready for Estelle and Mia to dance on the tables, and Jim had gone outside 'to get some air'.

'Stand around on the sports field looking shifty, more like,' Abs muttered, watching him through the window.

'Time Lord,' said Estelle, and I turned round to see him strolling in, carrying a newspaper and a huge cup of coffee.

Abs stood up and smoothed down her jeans. 'Let's do it.'

'Morning, all,' said Time Lord as the seven of us descended on him. He looked surprised, which was understandable considering the effort we'd put into avoiding him previously.

'Sir, we need to talk to you,' said Abs.

'It's important,' added Soph.

'Of course,' he said, sounding more surprised than ever.

We led him over to a quiet corner of the

canteen. I took Jim's phone out of my bag and launched into the story of how we knew Jim had lied about losing it.

'Rosie saw him put it in his pocket out on the field,' said Soph, 'and then there it was, behind the radiator.'

'I pulled the phone out, and we knew it was his because – well, obviously we'd seen it before,' I explained.

'Wait a minute,' said Time Lord. 'You're telling me this is Jim's phone?'

'Yes.'

'For the love of Shakespeare,' said Time Lord, thumping his fist on the table. 'Haven't I taught you anything? We had this discussion the last time you took it upon yourselves to walk off with Mr Falconer's phone.'

'But –' I protested.

'No, Rosie, there are no buts. You need to learn respect for other people's property.'

'Can I say something?' Leon asked.

'I . . . well . . . I suppose so,' said Time Lord.

'The girls reckon Jim's up to no good,' said Leon, 'and we think they might be right.' The others nodded. Leon grinned sheepishly in our direction. 'If you look at the text message they found on Jim's phone, the numbers are there in black and white.'

'It's a list of crate numbers,' I said, passing the phone to Time Lord. 'They match up with the ones you packed from the library.'

He read the message, but didn't say anything.

'We think Jim's planning to steal the computer equipment,' said Estelle.

'It doesn't make sense,' said Time Lord, although you could totally tell he was starting to believe us. 'Why would Jim do something so –'

'Stupid?' suggested Harris.

'Illegal?' said Abs.

'Reckless,' said Time Lord.

'We think he needs the money,' said Leon. '*Really* needs it.' And he told Time Lord about the phone calls he'd overheard.

'No.' Time Lord shook his head. 'Jim sorted

out backers a long time ago. Money's tight – that's why he's staying with me – but if he was seriously in debt, I'd know about it. He confides in me.'

'But don't you see, sir,' I said, deciding it was time to go for broke, 'he looks up to you. You're his mentor. Maybe he's embarrassed to admit to you that he's got money problems.'

'Yeah,' said Abs, who'd cottoned on. 'I bet he feels he's letting you down.'

'Especially as you brought him to Whitney High and suggested filming here,' I said.

'You could be right,' breathed Time Lord. 'It does all seem to fit together. And –'

He froze, and so did the rest of us.

Jim's phone was still sitting on the table and it had just started to ring.

Chapter Nine

The phone kept ringing as we stared at it.

'Should we answer it, d'you think?' said Soph.

'You do it,' I said, pushing the phone towards Time Lord.

'Me?' said Time Lord.

'Yeah,' said Leon. 'Pretend you're Jim.'

'*Act* like you're Jim,' I said.

Honestly, it's so easy to make Time Lord do stuff by sucking up to him. Maybe that's what Amanda Hawkins has been up to all this time.

'Go on, sir,' said Abs.

Time Lord was obviously weakening.

'I *suppose* I could.' He picked the phone up.

'You can do it,' said Estelle.

'Be Jim,' added Mia.

He pressed 'accept' and held the phone to his ear.

'Uh-huh . . . OK . . . yes . . . OK.'

'So?' I said, a few agonisingly silent seconds after he'd hung up.

Time Lord put the phone back down on the table, slowly and deliberately. 'The voice said, "Tonight's the night. The truck'll be there at nightfall".'

I had the feeling it was more information than any of us had really dared to expect. Like we'd suspected it might be Jim's mum on the phone, wanting to know if he'd washed behind his ears or something.

'What did he sound like?' I asked.

'Gruff,' said Time Lord. 'Like an uncouth yob.'

'I bet it was the same person who called before,' I said. 'He had a really rough voice, too.'

'Did he say anything else?' asked Leon.

'To make sure I've got an alibi – or rather, for Jim to make sure he's got one,' said Time Lord.

'Dude,' said Harris, shaking his head.

'It does look rather serious,' said Time Lord. 'I'm sorry I doubted you. What we're going to do about it all, I don't know.'

'Well, I think the last Justin Timberlake single rocked,' said Abs. 'He's a god.'

'Eh?' said Soph, and I felt Abs kick her under the table.

The rest of us looked confused. A second later, Jim walked through the canteen doors, a few feet away from where we were sitting. Abs had obviously seen him coming along the corridor.

'Absolutely, I agree,' said Time Lord, way too loudly, 'Jackson Lumberjack is excellent.'

Jim gave him an odd look, then walked across to where the cameras were set up and clapped his hands.

'Right,' he said. 'Let's get on, shall we?'

He called Mia and Estelle over, along with

Harris and Leon. Their characters came in at the end of the scene.

'Extras,' he called, a few minutes later, and gave us directions.

The scene started. Somehow, though, it was difficult to concentrate, and I knew the others felt the same. Estelle, who'd hardly got a line wrong since the start of the film, was doing an Amanda Hawkins (i.e. being hopeless), and every time Mia smiled it looked really forced. Leon and Harris missed their entrance twice, and Time Lord's hair was more loonissimo than ever.

'Will you please concentrate!' yelled Jim, eventually. 'I know today's the last day of filming, but I need you to keep it together until the end of the afternoon. Then we can relax.'

'The end of the afternoon, or nightfall?' Abs whispered.

* * *

It seriously felt like *months* before the end of the afternoon arrived. When Jim finally told us the last scene was a wrap (I am sooo getting good at this film lingo), everyone clapped and a few people looked misty-eyed. Jim gave a short speech about how much he appreciated everyone's help, and said he was going to arrange a special screening for us at Borehurst cinema when he'd finished editing the film. There was more clapping, then people started drifting towards the door.

'Where d'you reckon Time Lord went?' said Soph, bounding over to me and Abs.

She'd spotted Time Lord disappearing, just as me, Soph, Estelle, Leon and Mia had. I wasn't sure about Harris – he's very good at looking gorgeous, but totally hopeless at noticing stuff.

'I don't know,' said Abs.

'I tried to find out when he came back, but he went all stony-faced on me,' I said.

'By "tried to find out" she means she waggled her eyebrows up and down a bit,' Abs told Soph.

'Everyone knows what that means,' I protested. 'Leon and Estelle did it too, but he ignored us all.'

'He's over there,' said Soph, pointing. 'Let's ask him.'

We walked across to where Time Lord was pulling on his jacket, but just as we got near, Jim wandered over.

'Quick,' said Abs. She pulled me and Soph down on to a bench and started taking things out of her bag, as if she was looking for something.

'Er, Abs,' I said, with my nose squashed into her bag, 'what are we doing, exactly?'

'Listening,' she hissed. 'Sssshhhh.'

' . . . looking pretty good,' we heard Jim say to Time Lord.

'I'd say so,' Time Lord agreed.

'How about joining us for dinner?' said Jim. I glanced over and saw him patting Time Lord on the back. 'I'm taking some of the kids out to celebrate the last day of filming, and thought you might like to come along.'

'Absolutely,' said Time Lord. 'Terrific idea. Thanks.' He looked at his watch, then glanced quickly in our direction. 'I'll meet you back at the house,' he told Jim. 'I need to have a word with a couple of my year-nine girls. There's some extra holiday homework I need to give them.'

'No worries,' said Jim, clapping him on the back again. 'See you later.'

We watched as Jim rounded up Estelle, Leon, Harris and Mia. The five of them headed out to the car park. Time Lord beckoned us over.

'I can't wait around for long,' he said. 'I need to get home.'

'Where did you –' I began, but he held his hand up.

'I've tipped off the police,' he explained. 'That was where I went earlier. I spoke to an officer on the phone, gave him the address and told him the business is going down tonight.'

'The what?' said Abs.

'It's police-speak,' he said. 'It speeds things up. I was in an episode of *The Bill* once, so I know what I'm talking about. Anyway, they're going to catch the thieves red-handed. Apprehend them in the act. Land the fish, so to speak.'

'Do you mean,' I said, wondering how him talking gibberish was meant to speed things up, 'they believed you and they're coming to catch the criminals and stop them stealing the computer stuff?'

'Yes.'

'Wow,' said Abs.

'Hang on,' I said. 'Didn't you just agree to go out to dinner with Jim?'

'I did,' said Time Lord. 'It took some quick thinking, but I'm nothing if not sharp of wits.'

Or full of hot air, I managed not to say.

'It's perfect. I'll drive us all to the restaurant, make some excuse to stop off at the school on the way and be here when the police arrive,' he said, rubbing his hands together. 'And, of course, it'll drop Jim right in it.'

'I thought he was your friend,' said Abs.

'We were never that close,' said Time Lord. 'And the idea that I've been harbouring a criminal under my roof for the last month is not a happy one. No, I'll be glad to see him get what he deserves.'

We went back to my house after that. Time Lord dashed off to meet Jim at home, and we texted Leon and Estelle to tell them what was happening.

'Don't you look a happy bunch?' said Nan, as we spilled through the front door, talking excitedly.

'Nan!' I gave her a huge hug. 'You were right.'

'I usually am, dear,' she said. 'Would anyone like a cup of tea and a garibaldi? There's a fresh packet in the kitchen.'

We followed her, even though none of us actually likes garibaldis.

'You were right about Jim Falconer,' I tried again.

'What's he done?' said Nan, dropping her box of teabags. 'I knew there was something iffy going on.'

We filled her in on everything we'd found out, and how even the police believed us now. Honestly, I don't think I've ever seen her look so excited about something that wasn't related to biscuits or television.

'Fancy that,' she said for about the millionth time. 'I told you, didn't I? Never judge a book by its cover. All that commander equipment, just waiting to be stolen.'

'*Computer* equipment, Nan,' I grinned.

'We'd never have suspected him if you hadn't given us the idea, Mrs Parker,' said Soph.

'That's very kind of you, dear,' said Nan, patting Soph's hand.

'I wish Jim had invited us out to dinner,' said Abs. She was sitting cross-legged in one of the kitchen chairs with her chin in her hands.

'It would've been so cool to be there when Jim's arrested and see his face when he realises Time Lord stopped at school on purpose,' I agreed.

'We should do it!' said Nan.

Me, Abs and Soph looked at her blankly.

'Go to the school,' Nan explained. 'I can drive us there in your mum's car, and we'll watch the action as it happens.'

'Really?' I said.

'Of course,' said Nan. 'I'm not about to miss

the chance to see a real, live mystery being wrapped up, especially one we helped solve.'

'Mum would kill us,' I said. 'You and me, both grounded for a week at least.'

'Well, she's not here,' said Nan. 'And what the eye doesn't see, the heart doesn't grieve over.'

I guessed she meant to say we were doing it and we'd worry about Mum afterwards. Sometimes my nan seriously rocks.

Chapter Ten

'All set?' said Nan an hour later, as we piled into Mum's car.

'Yep,' said Abs.

'Si, si, signora,' said Soph.

My phone beeped as I pulled the passenger door shut. It was a text from Estelle.

On way in TL's car. J with us – seems v. nervy.
C U there. X

'This is it, then,' I said.

Nan crunched the gears and we pulled away. She really is a très rubbish driver.

'My stomach feels weird,' said Soph.

I knew what she meant. Even though it was exciting to think we'd solved the crime and the bad guys were about to get caught, I couldn't help being nervous. What if we'd got it wrong? The detectives in Nan's murder-mystery shows are always talking about not wasting police time and how they can send you to prison for doing it.

Abs's phone beeped. It was a text from Leon.

'Which way?' said Nan.

'Left,' I said. 'How can you not know that?'

'It's nearly dark,' she said. 'Things look different.'

'Is it dark enough to count as "nightfall", d'you think?' said Soph.

'It's OK,' said Abs. 'Leon and the others just arrived at school and there's no one else there yet. Time Lord told Jim he'd forgotten his wallet. He's gone off with Leon to pretend to look for the caretaker.'

✳ ✳ ✳

Five minutes later, we turned into Whitney Lane.

'Take a left here,' said Abs, pointing. 'That road goes round to the back of the sports field, and there are some trees we can park behind.'

'Good thinking, Batgirl,' I said. 'If Jim spots us, he's bound to think something fishy's going on.'

Nan drove to the end of the road, and pulled up where Abs had suggested. 'We'll stay in the car for now,' she said. 'It's not a bad view from here. Are those the crates over there?'

'Yep,' I said.

'And there's Time Lord's car,' said Abs. It was parked outside the main entrance and we could just make out four figures sitting inside. 'I wonder where Time Lord and Leon are.'

'And the police,' said Nan.

'They must be hiding,' I said. 'They want to catch them in the act.'

'Look,' said Soph, craning her neck. 'There's a truck-thingy turning into the entrance.'

'It's a flat-bed lorry,' said Nan, the crime expert. 'Plenty of room for those crates, and a winch to lift them.'

The lorry drove on to the sports field. I couldn't help wondering what Jim was thinking, stuck in the car with Estelle, Harris and Mia, watching his crime unfold.

'See,' said Nan. 'They're backing it up so the winch will reach.'

We watched for another minute, then two men jumped out of the lorry and walked towards the crates. They peered closely at a couple and I guessed they were checking the labels. The first man gestured to a third, who was still in the lorry, and the winch moved over the crates. The second man climbed on top of one and grabbed the winch, pulling it downwards.

'He's hooking it on,' said Nan wisely.

'How d'you know this stuff?' I said. 'Other people's nans do knitting and keep budgies. Why is mine an expert on crime?'

'What use are budgies?' said Nan. 'You watch, as soon as he's off there, the other one'll lift it up on the winch and it'll swing round on to the lorry.'

But for once she was wrong. The man *did* get

down, but the instant he was back on the ground, six policemen sprang out of the two nearest crates, and the floodlights on the sports field burst into life. The men made a run for it, one heading towards the entrance, another running straight for our hiding place. The third man yanked the lorry door open, jumped out and ran straight into Leon and Time Lord. They each grabbed one of the man's arms and forced him to the ground.

'Go, Time Lord!' said Soph, and we squealed with laughter.

'Over here!' shouted Nan, who'd wound her window down. She switched the headlights on and started tooting the horn. The man was nearly at the clump of trees now and he slowed down, confused by the noise and lights. The two policemen chasing him caught up with him and wrestled him to the ground.

The final man was still running. Now we weren't hiding any more, me, Abs and Soph scrambled out of the car and ran on to the sports field.

'There he is!' said Abs.

Mia, Harris and Estelle were heading for him and, spotting them, the man swerved around the side of the science block. While everyone's attention was diverted, the passenger door opened and Jim tried to make a run for it, too.

'Stop him!' I yelled across the field.

Harris turned round just in time and flung himself at Jim. He caught the back of his jacket, and as Jim tried to pull free, a police van screeched through the gates with its lights flashing and siren wailing. Realising there was no escape, Jim put his hands in the air, and Harris led him to the van.

'Got 'em all, Sarge,' called a policewoman, appearing with the final, handcuffed man.

'Thank goodness for that,' said Nan, and I jumped. She's like a ninja, the way she creeps up on you. 'We'd better go over and tell them what we know,' she said. 'They might want to take a statement.'

* * *

'So, who are you?' said one of the policemen. We

were crowded round the police cars with Time Lord, Leon, Mia, Harris and Estelle.

'Pamela Millicent Parker,' said Nan, 'of twenty-seven –'

'No, I mean, why are you here?' interrupted the officer. 'What's your connection to the crime?'

'My granddaughter and her friends solved it,' said Nan, proudly. 'Don't you want to take a statement?'

Me, Abs and Soph were busy hugging the others (except for Time Lord, obviously – that would be totally cringe-issimo) and talking excitedly about what had happened.

'I nearly stopped breathing when you caught that one coming out of the lorry,' Abs told Leon.

'It must've been weird watching with Jim in the car,' I said.

'Harris was so cool,' said Mia, squeezing his arm.

'Jim!' said Soph, and we all whipped round as a policeman brought him round to the front of the car.

'Why'd you do it, dude?' said Harris.

'I knew he was up to no good,' said Nan.

'Remember, Jim, anything you say can be taken down and used as evidence in a court of law,' said Time Lord.

'A bit of hush, please,' said the policeman, holding his hand up. 'And if you don't mind, sir,' he told Time Lord, 'I'll be the one reading him his rights. A bit part in *The Bill* does not make you a police officer.'

Time Lord's face went an odd purplish colour and he stopped talking.

'I think you owe these people an explanation, Mr Falconer,' the policeman continued.

Jim looked kind of squirmy. 'It's true. You trusted me, and I let you down. All I can say is I'm sorry. Truly sorry.'

'Why did you do it?' said Leon.

'Loan sharks,' said Jim. 'I had to borrow money to make the film and I thought the bank would lend it to me. When they said no, I was desperate. I couldn't let the one chance I had to make a hit movie slip through my fingers. These crooks,' he spat, indicating the three men sitting handcuffed in the police van, 'are always on the lookout for an easy victim, and I fell for their offer. When I couldn't keep up with the repayments, I arranged for them to take the computer equipment in return for what I owed them. The crates, the labels, making sure everything was left on the sports field so they could get to it – I organised it all. I even told the caretaker to leave the gates open so I could shoot some night scenes.'

Nan tutted loudly behind me, and Time Lord shook his head in disgust. All around, I could see shocked faces.

'Come on,' said the policeman who was holding Jim. He opened the door of the nearest car and bundled him inside.

'Jim Falconer, a crook,' said Time Lord, still shaking his head as the police vehicles pulled away. 'If only he'd listened to me and gone into teaching.'

* * *

The rest of the holidays were pretty quiet. Soph

went to Italy with her mum and dad, Abs and her family went camping and I got to stay at home with Mum and Nan, being forced to watch *Diagnosis Murder* and listen to Bananarama CDs. It was odd though. After the excitement of the filming, then foiling Jim and the loan sharks, I sort of didn't mind getting back to normal. The only thing I really missed was hanging out with Estelle and the others. She sent me a few emails and I knew Leon and Abs were texting each other, but it wasn't the same.

When the beginning of the new school year rolled around, it felt really strange going back without the cameras being there.

'It's weird to think this was a film set a few weeks ago,' said Soph, as we filed into the hall for assembly on the first day back.

'Settle down,' shouted Meanie Greenie over the clatter of everyone taking their seats.

'Totally back to normal, then,' Abs whispered.

'Before we start,' said Meanie Greenie, 'I've got a few special announcements to make. As I'm sure you know, Whitney High was used as the setting for a film over the holidays. What you might not know is that the school was also the scene of an attempted theft.'

There were a few 'oohs' and 'blimeys' and 'no ways' before the hall fell silent again.

'Fortunately,' she continued, 'the attempt was unsuccessful, thanks to a member of staff and several students.'

She called our names and, blushing like mad, as the rest of the school applauded, me, Abs and Soph made our way up to stand on stage next to Time Lord and Meanie Greenie.

'Thanks to the intelligence, courage and –' Meanie grinned ' – good old-fashioned nosiness of these students, we still have our computer equipment.'

More clapping.

'In the light of this,' Meanie went on, 'I'm thrilled to present Rosie, Abigail and Sophie with tickets to the exclusive, and I'm sure very glamorous, première of *Pulse*. Miss Mayor and her co-stars took the film to another movie company and Mr Lord informs me it was snapped up immediately,' she explained. 'For those of you not attending the premiere, I understand the film will be coming to Borehurst in October.'

As everyone cheered, I caught sight of Amanda Hawkins sitting between Lara and Keira. She was so furious, there was practically smoke coming out of her nose.

'And speaking of Mr Lord,' Meanie Greenie said, once the cheering died down, 'I'd also like to recognise his part in foiling the theft.'

Miss Chapman, the school secretary, trotted over and handed her a package. Meanie passed it to Time Lord and shook his hand.

'I'm told by your colleagues it might be useful,' she said, as he unwrapped a brand-new shiny leather autograph book.

I stifled a giggle, and felt Abs do the same. We needn't have bothered, though – people all around the hall were sniggering and laughing.

'We're most grateful to all of you,' said Meanie

Greenie, and with one last round of applause, we followed Time Lord off the stage.

'How exciting,' he whispered.

'It's so cool they found someone to take on the film,' I said.

'Indeed,' said Time Lord. 'And the good news is I'll be going to the première, too.'

'You'll be able to use your autograph book,' said Soph.

Time Lord shuffled his feet awkwardly. 'About that,' he said. 'Now you're all film stars, or about to be anyway, I was wondering if the three of you would . . . er . . . sign it for me.'

Me, Abs and Soph looked at each other, then burst out laughing. Film stars? Autographs? Talk about a summer we'd never forget.

Time Lord passed me the book, and I wrote:

To Mr L.
See you at the premiere!
Best wishes,
Rosie Parker (actress, mystery-solver, superstar)

Tim Lord's Top Ten of Acting

1. Don't make a fuss if you don't get the part you hoped for. True actors do not break down in tears when they find out that their arch-enemy got the main part.

2. If there's any food on the stage, don't be tempted to have a nibble. It could be covered in varnish, made of plastic—or worse!

3. Always learn your lines inside out and back to front. Forgetting them can make a director very annoyed. I learned that the hard way.

4. You must live and breathe your part. When I played a Cyberman in *Doctor Who*, I wore my mask everywhere I went for a month beforehand. Mind you, the ladies in the supermarket didn't like it much, and it gave my poor old Mum a real fright.

5. No matter how many times your fellow actors tell you that the greasepaint make-up tastes like bubblegum, DO NOT believe them and lick it. They are pulling your leg! I also learned this the hard way.

6. Do not start offering people your autograph before you have been given a part. No one is going to be impressed when they find out they have got the autograph of a silent scarecrow or an injured mouse.

7. If you're playing the part of a swamp monster/old tramp/alien, don't try and sweet talk the make-up lady into making you look beautiful or handsome. It won't work.

8. Don't be tempted to borrow your costume. The costume lady never forgave me when my Cyberman mask ended up full of custard when I borrowed it for the weekend.

9. Never say, 'Good luck' before a performance. We actors say, 'Break a leg' instead. Not that that did me much good when I was in *Jack and the Beanstalk*. I fell down the beanstalk halfway through and, you guessed it, broke my leg.

10. Make sure you stand in the right place when the curtain falls at the end. You don't want to be the only person on the wrong side of the curtain, trapped on the stage on your own in front of hundreds of people. Believe me, I've been there ...

Fact File

NAME: Estelle Mayor

AGE: 18

STAR SIGN: Taurus

HAIR: Long, dark and shiny

LOVES: Veggie food. Before she was a megastar, Estelle worked in a burger bar. She's gone right off burgers since she worked there!

HATES: Getting stage fright. She seems like a natural-born superstar, but even Estelle gets the jitters sometimes!

LAST SEEN: Hanging out with Rosie, Soph and Abs in Trotters. She might be a celeb star but she's not too good for a hot chocolate and a girlie natter!

MOST LIKELY TO SAY: 'I'll buy you a blueberry muffin if you help me learn my lines'

WORST CRINGE EVER: Picking up her gym bag instead of her costume on the way to an audition. Singing show tunes dressed in an old T-shirt, holey shorts and stinky trainers is sooo not a good look!

Megastar

Everyone has blushing blunders - here are some from your Megastar Mysteries friends!

Rosie Parker

Everyone was really excited about being invited to the party at the end of filming *Pulse* – the wrap party. It's called that because it's held after the filming has been wrapped up (finished). But muggins here didn't know that. I thought it was called a rap party, because there was going to be rap music playing. It's lucky for me we found out that Jim Falconer is a crook and the party was cancelled, otherwise I would have been the wally break-dancing to Beyoncé. Cringe-a-rama!

Pam Parker

We were sitting in the car waiting for the police to catch that rotten Jim Falconer and the girls were giggling in the back seat about how that young Leon seems to have a soft spot for Abigail. Suddenly, Jim Falconer ran out right in front of my car and the policeman shouted, 'Stop that Nan!' I stuck my head out of the window and shouted back, 'You leave me out of this!' I couldn't understand why everyone looked so surprised until I realised that he had said, 'Stop that MAN' not, 'Stop that NAN'!

Cringes

Harris

I know it sounds a bit silly, but ever since I was about five I've been really scared of cats. I don't like them and they don't like me. If there's a cat around I know I'm going to end up getting scratched to pieces. So when we'd finished filming a scene of *Pulse* in the school kitchen and Jim Falconer shouted 'Cut!' at the end, I leapt of my skin and sent a whole rack of plates crashing to the floor. You guessed it – I thought he'd shouted 'Cat!' and was flailing around madly trying to avoid the furry little fiend!

Sophie McCoy

Estelle admired one of my fashion creations, so I thought I would customise something for her as a surprise. I grabbed all of my crafty bits and made a hair band covered in shiny red ribbon and sequins for her. She loved it so much that she asked the stylist if she could wear it in the movie. It looked totally awesome in her dark hair until it started to pour with rain and red dye ran down her face! She had to have her make-up redone and a whole scene had to be filmed again. Blushville Central or what?!

Estelle Mayor

I got up really late one morning and didn't have time for breakfast before filming began. I was sooo hungry by about ten o'clock that when I saw a cream bun sitting on the table, I couldn't help myself and just had to have a bite. Little did I know that Jim Falconer always has a special cream bun every day. When he came to get his mid-morning snack he went absolutely mad, screaming about someone stealing it! I went so red and, to make things worse, I had a splodge of cream on my nose so there was no hiding that it was me!

Tim Lord's autograph book

Check out Mr Lord's, erm, 'famous' friends!

Mr Lord, I will never grumble about drama class again. Bet you'd never thought you'd see ME on the big screen, eh?! Rosie (superstar – and super sleuth!)

Thanks for everything you taught me, Mr L!
Estelle Mayor

Amanda Hawkins

Mandy H

Miss A Hawkins

What am I supposed to be doing? Is this a test? I don't get it . . . Harris

Ooh, you're a lovely young man. My daughter is looking for love you know. Why don't you come round and get to know each other better over a nice cup of tea and a Bourbon?
Yours sincerely, Pam Parker

Mr Lord and my mum?! Not if I can help it! Rosie

Now that I've made my acting debut, it's next stop Doctor Who. Ex-ter-min-ate! Ex-ter-min-ate! Abs

Soph's Style Tips

If pocket money is tight but you want a fab new look, try sticking on a hat!

WOOLLY WONDERS

Try customising a beanie for some cheap and chic cosiness!
- Pin on some badges for a rock-chick look
- Add a brooch to look ladylike
- Sew on some buttons for a cute touch!

A HELPING HAT

You can find cheap 'n' chic hats just waiting to be customised here:

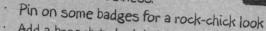

☑ CHARITY SHOPS
☑ SUPERMARKET CLOTHING DEPARTMENTS
☑ HIDING IN THE BOTTOM OF YOUR WARDROBE!

SOPH'S TOP HATS

1 Beanie - the ultimate bad hair disguise!
2 Beret - so French, so chic. Ooh, la, la!
3 Baseball cap - even I can pretend to be sporty sometimes!

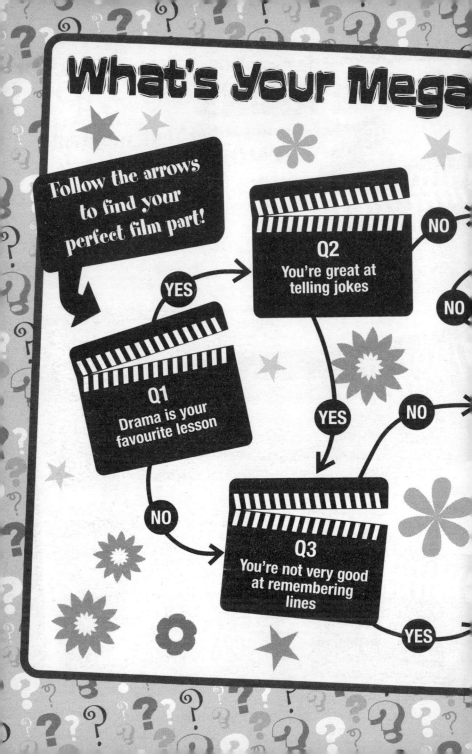

Movie Role?

YES

Q4
School play?
No way!
Agree?

YES

Q5
You dream of seeing your name in lights

NO

NO

YES

Q6
The best part of being in a play is the party afterwards

YES

Shining Superstar

Were you born wearing massivo sunglasses and a feather boa, signorina? Cos it seems like you were made to be a leading lady! You love learning lines, and song-and-dance routines are pretty much your fave thing ever. Your mates think you've got star potential and can't wait to go to your first premiere!

NO

Comedy Cutie

Heavy dramas aren't your thing, but anything that involves dressing up in a crazissimo costumes, throwing custard pies or tripping over your own feet is right up your street! You don't care about looking a fool on stage cos you just love making people laugh. That means you're amazing fun to hang out with too, and your friends love you for it.

Excellent Extra

OK, so you might not be a gifted actress but you've got enthusiasm by the bucketload, and that's what counts, right? You're not bothered about being a star, you just like to be involved (and to have a guaranteed invite to the cast party!). Drama classes are a great excuse to catch up on the latest gossip with your pals — oh, and to occasionally brush up on those useful acting skills!

♥ ♥ Find Your Star Name!

Reckon you'll be a celeb one day? Find your film star name here!

What to do:

Look up the first letter of your first name on the first list. The word next to it is your movie star first name. Then go to the second list and look up the first letter of your surname – et voilà! You have your film star name! It's time to start practising your signature, cos you're now a movie star. Brillissimo!

First names	
A	Sugar
B	Mercedes
C	Opal
D	Dream
E	Champagne
F	Paris
G	Estelle
H	Crystal
I	Princess
J	Shimmer
K	Silver
L	Violet
M	Paige
N	Ruby
O	Mirage
P	Flame
Q	Shelby
R	Bubbles
S	Fifi
T	Angel
U	Stardust
V	Peaches
W	Hollie
X	Lily-Rose
Y	Amber
Z	Trixie

Second name	
A	Bon-Bon
B	Comet
C	St Claire
D	Sequin
E	Sparkles
F	L'Amore
G	Hollywood
H	Gemstone
I	Boulevard
J	Brilliant
K	Jacuzzi
L	Goldings
M	Glimmer
N	Diva
O	Cashmere
P	Galore
Q	Fame
R	Galaxy
S	Harlequin
T	Tinsel
U	Rouge
V	Glam
W	Diamond
X	Sweetland
Y	Starr
Z	Blaze

Pam's Problem Page

Never fear, Pam's here to sort you out!

Dear Pam,

I'm in a ton of trouble. I borrowed some money and I can't afford to pay it back. Now the men who lent it to me are getting a bit threatening and I don't know what to do. Can you help me come up with a scam to make a lot of money and get myself out of this mess?

Jim

Pam says: A SCAM? Ooh, you've got a cheek, young man. In all her years, Murder, She Wrote's Jessica Fletcher never once got on the wrong side of the law and I'm not about to do so either. Good grief, I think I need to make myself a nice cup of tea to calm down. You were silly enough to borrow all of that money, and you can find a way to pay it back. Try buying the cheaper kind of garibaldi biscuits for a while. You'll be surprised how quickly those saved pennies add up and you'll be able to pay back the money in no time. And if those men give you any more nonsense, why not invite them round to watch a spot of Miss Marple? You'll soon be the best of friends.

Can't wait for the next
book in the series?
Here's a sneak preview of

Amber

AVAILABLE NOW
from all good bookshops, or
www.mega-star.co.uk

Chapter One

It was a wet Saturday afternoon, I had a massive zit on my nose and huge piles of homework to do. Yet this was possibly one of the most exciting days of my life! No, I wasn't in some kind of parallel universe, like in *Doctor Who*. I was excited because me, Soph and Abs were about to win a radio competition to meet The Gems!

The Gems were this totally hot new band from near Borehurst. The three girls in the band talked Girl Power, but you knew they really meant it; they wouldn't stab each other in the back over a hot boy. These girls were mates, through and through – they had been since the first day of school, kind of like me, Abs and Soph. Maybe that's why we liked them. Anyway, we were totally about to win – live on air!

'Stop hogging the phone,' Abs hissed at me. The three of us were squidged together on my bed, trying to listen to my mobile.

'Owww!' shrieked Soph as her humongous silver clip-on earring got caught in my phone charm.

'Sssh!' I said, untangling her. 'We won't hear when they call us!'

'Let's go to line two, to Rosie, Sophie and Abs!' the DJ said. 'Hello there!'

I gave a mini-scream as Abs and Soph calmly said, 'Hello.'

'So, you want to win a chance to interview The Gems, do ya?' he asked. 'Live on Fleetwich FM – the focal vocals for all funky folks!'

I rolled my eyes. Why do all local radio DJs have to be so cheesy? 'Yes please!' I said politely.

'Right! Well, answer this question: where did The Gems get their name?'

We looked at each other. This was so easy. 'Amber is a type of gem, and she's the lead singer,' Abs said coolly.

There was a pause. 'So, you're saying it's cos the lead singer's name is a kind of gemstone . . .?' the DJ began.

Hel-*lo*? Wasn't that what Abs said? 'Yes!' I said firmly.

'Well,' he said. 'I can tell you that . . .'

We were squeezing each other's hands.

'. . . you're right!!' he finally shouted.

We dropped the phone and leapt up, squealing and laughing. We'd won! We were going to meet The Gems!!

Soph did a mad dance involving lots of kicking legs (not ideal, as both her shoes flew off and hit me and Abs). Abs jumped up and down. I just screamed and screamed.

'Rosie, what is going on?' Mum had appeared at my bedroom door. She stared at Abs and Soph, who were now hugging each other.

'I thought there'd been a murder!' Nan said from behind Mum, panting from rushing upstairs.

I shook my head, too out of breath to explain.

'I guess that means you're happy. Ha ha!' the DJ quacked from my mobile, abandoned on the bed. 'Fleetwich FM aims to please . . .'

We all scrabbled for the phone.

'Hello, hi, sorry about that!' I gabbled, waving madly at Abs and Soph to shut the door and get rid of Mum and Nan.

'Well done!' the DJ cried cheerily. 'Stay on the line and we'll make arrangements. Here's the latest song from The Gems themselves – "Crystal Clear".'

As it started to play, he transferred me to a producer and I gave her my details. By this time, Soph and Abs were back.

'The interview will be next Saturday at eleven a.m.,' the producer said.

'Next Saturday at eleven,' I repeated, looking at Soph and Abs. Abs nodded immediately, but

Soph looked agonised before nodding too. 'Great! See you then. Thanks!'

'What's up, Soph?' I asked, ringing off.

'I'm supposed to be working next Saturday.'

Soph has this weekend job in Dream Beauty, a beauty salon in Borehurst. She's always moaning about it but she needs the money. She is obsessed with clothes. Not your common-or-garden designer gear – her own creations. She gets stuff from charity shops and customizes it in totally bizarre ways that somehow work (on her, anyway). Stuff from charity shops doesn't exactly cost the earth, but let's just say Soph can buy a LOT on a shopping trip. Never underestimate the fashionista-sista side of her.

'Can't you get the day off?' Abs asked.

'I have to, but Mrs Blessing will kill me,' Soph said.

'Well, you work on her, and I'll persuade Mum to drive us,' I said. 'Oh, hi, Mum.'

She'd opened the door again. 'That was pretty loud screaming, girls. How do you fancy being backing singers for the Banana Splits?'

I shuddered. Mum's Bananarama tribute band is cringe-worthy enough without actually performing with them. But if that was what it would take to get her to drive us to Fleetwich FM, I'd leap into some spandex leggings in a heartbeat.

* * *

On Wednesday morning, Soph was beaming. 'I've got the day off on Saturday!'

'How'd you wangle that?' I asked.

'I'm working the next three Fridays after school.'

'Brilliant!' Abs said.

Just then, Amanda Hawkins the class witch sneered into view. 'Are the Tragic Trio having fun?'

'We're just talking about meeting The Gems on Saturday,' Abs said. 'Cos we won that competition. To meet The Gems.'

'Whatever,' Amanda said, storming off. 'Losers.'

'Er, winners, I think you'll find,' I called after her. Somehow, Amanda being hacked off made me even happier.

The Gems were even mentioned in *Star Secrets* that week. They'd been at a party with Poppy Carlton, the winner of *Teen Town*, the teen reality show that was massive last summer. She's always in the goss mags, partying and clubbing, even though she's only sixteen. Soph is sooo jealous of her because she's always got the latest hot bag or shoes. The Gems were hitting the big time!

※ ※ ※

That Saturday, thanks to my marvelloso persuasive powers (and promising to go to the next Banana Splits gig), Mum was driving me, Abs and Soph to Fleetwich FM. Unfortunately, she was also singing along to the radio très loudly.

'You know I want yoooo-ou, you know I need yoooo-ou!'

'Mu-um!'

Abs and Soph winced in sympathy.

'You're the only one! You're no lonely one!'

I tried to turn the radio down.

'Ooh no, I like this one, Rosie. Leave it on. Ah, here we are.'

Sacrebleu.

We turned up a lane that led to a large building. It looked totally ordinary. Who'd have thought some soon-to-be megastars were waiting inside – for us!

'Come on!' Soph was already out of the car.

'Call me when you're done,' Mum said.

Nervously, we walked into the totally featureless reception area.

'Er, we're here to interview The Gems,' I said to the security guard. 'We're the winners. You know, of the competition. On Fleetwich FM. Obviously.'

'Sign there, please,' he said in a bored tone. He told us to take the lift to the fifth floor.

It was a bit livelier up there. Music pumped from speakers and as the lift doors opened, a funky-looking girl in shorts and boots approached us.

'I'm Jenny. Are you the competition-winners?'

'Yup!' Abs said.

'Follow me. You're on in fifteen minutes.'

We followed Jenny down the corridor and into a room filled with comfy sofas.

'Danny Darwin will be ready for you soon,' Jenny said.

We sat down to wait.

'So, have you got your list of questions, Rosie?' Abs asked.

'Bien sûr, ma soeur,' I replied. A good journalist – which is what I'm going to be one day – is always prepared. I opened my notebook.

Question One, it said. And that was all. I remembered now – Nan had called me to sort out the Sky Plus for her and I'd never carried on! Aargh.

Abs and Soph were looking at me expectantly. I could see they'd both written loads.

'Er, yes,' I said. 'Lots of questions here.' Well, a good journalist also knows how to think on her feet.

Just then, there was a knock on the door. The Gems had arrived! Amber, the lead singer, bounded in first. She had long blonde hair and wore jeans and a funky yellow top. Rachel and Carly weren't far behind. They both wore très cool shirtdresses, one white, one green. Rachel had short brown hair and Carly had her black hair scraped back in a ponytail. They all grinned as they shook our hands.

'Nice to meet you,' Amber said.

'It's such a pleasure to meet you,' I gushed.

'I love your hairband,' Amber said to Soph, who beamed. She'd added some sequins to an Alice band and it was her new fave thing to wear.

'It's really cool we're being interviewed by three friends,' Rachel said.

'Yeah,' Carly agreed. 'It's so appropriate!'

'Right, in you come, girls,' Jenny said. 'This way.'

We all followed Jenny to a door marked Studio 1. Behind it was a large room with a massive desk covered in buttons and slidey things and lights. I seriously wanted to fiddle with them, but realised a serious journalist would not behave like an idiot. Chairs stood around a table with a microphone on it. Danny Darwin, the DJ, took off his headphones to say hello.

Jenny showed us where to sit at the table. Amber smiled at me as I sat next to her. She was so nice!

Danny turned the music down. 'And in two minutes we'll be talking to The Gems, so stay tuned!' Then he flicked a switch and some adverts came on. 'Right, ladies,' he said, turning to us. 'Ready?'

We looked at each other and nodded. My throat had suddenly got very dry.

'So, here we are with The Gems,' Danny said, 'and our competition-winners, Sophie, Abs and Rosie are running the show. Take it away, girls!'

'So,' I said nervously, 'how long have you been in the band?'

'A few years,' Rachel replied. 'Since we left school, we've been playing at youth clubs, shopping centres and school fêtes.'

'And now we've got a deal with this massive record label!' Carly said.

Amber looked at her mates. 'Yup. They say we're going to be huge.' She didn't look happy though.

'Did they hear you play somewhere?' Abs asked.

'Our manager – Amber's dad – had sent them a demo CD. A scout came to watch us at the mall in Borehurst,' Rachel said.

Soph was next. 'If you were an item of clothing, what would you be?'

The Gems looked a little startled. Then they grinned.

'Ballet pumps,' Carly said. 'They're girly and sweet, like me!'

'I'd be a charm bracelet,' Rach said. 'It's dainty and looks good on someone's arm.'

Amber snorted and tried to turn it into a cough.

'Ooh, whose arm would you like to be on?' I asked Rach quickly.

'Well, mine, obviously,' Danny interjected. The girls all laughed.

'How about you, Amber?' Soph asked.

'I'd have to say some vintage boots. Because I'm individual, hard-working and totally rock 'n' roll.'

I couldn't help thinking it was an odd thing for a member of a pop group to say.

Abs chimed in with her next question, but I was distracted. There was definitely something weird about Amber. Why did I feel that The Gems weren't such close friends after all?